YOU CALL THE

Help to put Mountain Mike behind bars . . .
Enter a huckleberry pie-eating contest . . .
Risk your life to stop a train robbery . . .
Win Heartland's annual "suicide race" . . .

What happens in this book is up to you, according to the choices you make, page by page. You'll find over thirty possible endings, from scary to serious to surprising. And it all starts with an innocent cross-country train ride. . . .

MAKING Choices

TIME WARP TUNNEL

By Stephen A. Bly

Chariot Books™
A Division of Cook Communications

JF
Bly

For my buddy, Aaron

Chariot Books™ is an imprint of David C. Cook Publishing Co.
David C. Cook Publishing Co., Elgin, Illinois 60120
David C. Cook Publishing Co., Paris, Ontario
Nova Distribution Ltd., Eastbourne, England

TIME WARP TUNNEL
©1985 by Stephen A. Bly

Originally published as *TROUBLE IN QUARTZ MOUNTAIN TUNNEL*

Cover design by Jack Foster
Cover illustration by Dave Joly
Interior illustrations by VanSeveren
First printing as *Time Warp Tunnel*, 1994
Printed in the United States of America
98 97 96 95 94   5 4 3 2 1

Library of Congress Cataloging in Publication Data
Bly, Stephen A.
    Time warp tunnel.
    (A Making Choices Book)
    Summary: After a train enters a tunnel and emerges in the Wild West of the
1880s, the reader makes decisions determining the course of the story.
    1. Children's stories, American. 2. Plot-your-own stories. [1. West (U.S.)—Fiction.
2. Space and time—Fiction. 3. Plot-your-own stories]
I. VanSeveren, Joe, Ill. II. Title.
PZ7l.B6275Tr 1985 [Fic] 84-23871
ISBN 0-7814-0187-9

CAUTION!

This is not a normal book! If you read it straight through, it won't make sense.

Instead, you must start at page 1 and then turn to the pages where your choices lead you. One moment you're on the Amtrak, entering the Quartz Mountain Tunnel, and the next moment you find yourself transported back in time to the very Wild West. From then on, your decisions can lead you into exciting and dangerous escapades in a world you'd only read about before.

If you want to read this book, you must choose to
Turn to page 1.

"Hey! What happened?" you hear someone yell.

Then you recognize the voice—it's your own!

A moment ago you were lazily gazing out the Amtrak window at the Rocky Mountain countryside. Then everything turned dark. Real dark.

You can't see a thing out the window. You can't even see the window.

"Relax, kid," you hear someone behind you reply. "It's just the north end of the Quartz Mountain Tunnel."

Then suddenly, wham! Light slams against your eyelids.

"Wow! That was some tunnel," you say, turning to the family sitting behind you, who had earlier introduced themselves as the Pratts from St. Louis.

But the Pratt family has disappeared. And in their place sits . . .

Turn to page 2.

. . . a man wearing an old buckskin jacket. A lady next to him wears a long, old-fashioned dress and bonnet. The train itself looks very different. It looks so . . . so antique.

I'm dreaming, you think.

Just as you're about to say something, the train slows and comes to a screeching halt. You swing back toward the window. You've entered a town. The sign on the depot reads Heartland.

"I don't remember any Heartland on this route," you ponder.

The town looks strange. No paved streets. No cars. No TV aerials. No streetlights. Just plenty of horses, buggies, and people dressed up as though they were in a western movie, walking around on wooden sidewalks.

Someone taps your shoulder. "You'll have to get off here. Your ticket's good only to Heartland." You turn to stare at a train official.

"But there must be a mistake," you stammer. "I'm going to my aunt's house in Anaheim. I'm going to see the Dodgers and Disneyland and surf on the beach. . . ."

"Come on, kid, don't mumble," the conductor says roughly. "You've got to get off here."

Choices: You meekly get off the train (turn to page 3).
You insist that you're not getting off (turn to page 4).

You search frantically for a telephone booth so you can call your dad. Not seeing one, you run over to the man at the ticket counter. As you step in line, you notice a girl about your age staring at your shoes.

"Are those moccasins?" she says.

"They're tennis shoes, of course," you reply. "Nikes, to be exact."

"Look like cheap moccasins to me," she sneers.

You ignore her as your turn at the ticket counter comes. "Excuse me, sir," you say politely, "where's the nearest phone I could use?"

"Excuse me?"

"I need a telephone. I want to call my dad," you repeat.

"Oh, you mean a telegraph? Sure, we got one. You want to send a message?"

"Don't tell me this town doesn't have a single telephone. Surely even a boonie town like this would . . ."

"Listen, kid, you're wasting my time. It's the Fourth of July, you know. We're busy. Now, do you want to use the telegraph?"

"Er, yeah, I guess so," you mumble. "Can you cash a traveler's check?"

"I only take gold and silver coins," he says, looking at you strangely. "Maybe you'd better head for the bank. Two blocks north, one block east. Next?"

Turn to page 5.

"Kid, we don't take kindly to panhandlers," the big man growls as he grabs the back of your collar. He starts to drag you toward the exit of the car you're in. You kick him in the shins, and he lets go his grip.

You run wildly to the back of the train and dive into the baggage car to hide. A large wooden crate is standing up against one side of the train car. It's marked Webber Cattle Company. You notice that the top is loose.

On the far side of the car you spot a large, open barrel with a bright pink label: Madame Peer's Emporium.

Choices: You jump into the crate (turn to page 10).
You push your way through to the barrel (turn to page 6).

As you walk through Heartland, you can't help but stare everywhere at once. It's all so weird—like walking back into history. "It's more like the 1880s than the 1980s," you say to yourself.

Just then, three men on horseback fly down the street, wildly firing guns in the air. You duck behind a stagecoach. They pass you, and you hear a loud commotion from the direction they're headed.

Choices: **You decide to follow carefully after the gunmen (turn to page 9).**
You run as fast as you can toward the bank (turn to page 8).

The barrel is full to the brim with wadded-up newspapers and old rags, but there's room for you to squeeze in.

Soon, you hear men talking close to you. You feel them lift the barrel.

Choices: **You holler, "Let me out of here!" (turn to page 42).**
You keep quiet and hope for a chance to escape (turn to page 7).

"This barrel sure is heavy," you hear a man complain.

You sit very still. After a few moments, bumpy movements suggest that you're riding in a wagon or something like it.

"Take it easy, Darrin," someone shouts. "You'll lose the whole load."

He's right. The barrel tips, rolls, and crashes to the ground, spilling you out. You feel dizzy as daylight nearly blinds you. You blink your eyes hard in time to see a wagon pulling to a stop in a cloud of dust. You turn for a quick look around. There's a creek nearby, with brush on the banks that you could hide in. As you race toward it, you stumble over a funny black box.

Choices: **You ignore the black box and keep racing for cover (turn to page 12).**
You pause to pick up the black box and then run for the brush (turn to page 62).

As you speed toward the bank, you try to remember if the man said two blocks down or one. You stop to peek into a store, in hopes of asking more directions, and someone cries out, "There you are! Your ma's been looking all over for you. You'd better hurry right down to the livery 'fore she has a mind to bust your britches." The shopkeeper gives you a shove with his broom.

"But I, I . . ." you begin.

"Go on, shoo! I don't want you Thomason kids hanging around here when the parade starts," he continues.

You scoot out of the way. As you walk past an alley, a lady motions you over. It's the woman who was sitting behind you on the train where Mrs. Pratt was supposed to be. "What's the matter?" she inquires.

"I don't know," you pout, hoping you don't break down and cry. "Everything's so confusing around here. I need to get to Anaheim. I need to call my dad. I need to . . ."

"Honey, don't you pay them no mind," she comforts. "The whole town's loco. Been that way for years. Why don't you come with us? We'll put you back on the train down at Reid City, and you can go wherever you want. How's that sound?"

Choices: You go with the woman (turn to page 45).

You explain that you've got to go to the bank first (turn to page 48).

As you round a corner, trailing after the shooting cowboys, a crowd gathers near the door of the Heartland Mercantile Company. Someone shrieks, "Fight! Fight!"

You can't see anything from where you stand.

Choices: **You climb up on a nearby horse to get a better view (turn to page 32).**
You climb a ladder to a balcony (turn to page 25).

What a dumb thing to do. The bottom of the crate is covered with . . .

"Oh, no!" you squeal, holding your nose. There, standing next to you in the crate, is a four-foot-high baby buffalo. It doesn't move. In the poor light of the crate, the animal seems to have a sickly, dazed look in his eyes.

"Poor thing," you say to it. "Why would anyone want to crate you up like this?"

The thought hits you that the buffalo needs some fresh air (and so do you)—quick. With great caution, you open the crate. You see two men unloading the barrel, so you wait for them to leave. Then you explore the car for a way of escape. The side door is bolted down. You can't return through the passenger car, or the conductor might find you.

You find a crowbar. You intend to break open the side of the car, but your conscience stops you. *This is private property,* you remind yourself. *What do you think you're doing?*

Choices: **You shake the thought off and break down the door (turn to page 11).**
You pray, "Lord, what should I do now?" (turn to page 34).

The lock breaks off with just a few hard jabs. You slide the door open and gaze around at the peaceful surroundings. Then you return to the crate and break it open.

Surprised by his sudden freedom, the buffalo tramples over most of the baggage in the car. You find it difficult to coax him to the open door. You're afraid to push him from behind, and equally wince at pulling him from the front. Most of your strategy consists of hissing, "Scram! Scram!"

All of a sudden the train lurches forward. You slip and fall on top of the baggage. The panicked buffalo bolts toward the open door—only you're in front of it.

You're about to fall victim to a one-buffalo stampede.

Choices: You scramble out the side door of the moving train, just ahead of the buffalo (turn to page 40).

You shut your eyes tight and pray that God will forgive every rotten thing you've done (turn to page 71).

You watch two men scurry back through the dust to pick up the pieces of the barrel.

"You're mighty lucky the whole thing didn't blow up," one says.

"Naw, it couldn't. Not until they're mixed together, anyway," the other answers.

"Ain't nothin' here but some old rags and papers," the first one states.

"Over there, Darrin. Don't you 'magine that's what she wants? The black box. She claims it'll change the course of history."

"Grab it, and let's git to Dusty Springs Ranch."

The wagon is loaded with other boxes. You notice a bit of room at the back that perhaps you could sneak into.

Choices: **You make a leap for the wagon when the men aren't looking (turn to page 49).**

You forget the box and the wagon and hike back to town (turn to page 13).

You're not far from town and the train track. You walk until you reach the station. "Boy, oh boy," you say to yourself. "They don't even have indoor plumbing!"

You march back into the train and sit down. *I'm not getting off this train till I reach Anaheim,* you determine.

No sooner have you made your decision than a loud explosion propels you out of your seat. You and several other passengers fight to get out the door.

Choices: You shove a lady in front of you to one side and jump onto the platform (turn to page 15).

You let the others go first and crawl under a seat for protection (turn to page 14).

After the commotion dies down, you discover a couple of boys setting off firecrackers. When they see you've found them out, they climb out of the car, and you return to your seat. This time you're more determined than ever to stay put until you reach California.

The train pulls away from the station. The conductor soon walks through and asks for your ticket. Since he took it from you earlier, you have nothing to show him.

He pulls the emergency cord, and the train grinds to a stop. You run out the rear of the car. The next car, the baggage car, is locked, so you climb up a little ladder on the outside that leads to the top of the car. You stand up on top and wait a moment. The conductor doesn't seem to be following you.

All of a sudden the train lurches forward again. In the distance, you think you see another tunnel.

Choices: You decide to crawl back down the ladder and face the conductor (turn to page 16).

You stay where you are and lie flat (turn to page 18).

Once you're far enough away, you look back at the train. Two boys, about your age, emerge from the car laughing and pointing in your direction. They're holding what's left of a string of firecrackers.

"Did you see that kid? That was the really funny part," the fat one hoots.

"Yeah," says the other one. "What kind of kid would push down an old lady just to get out of the way of a couple of measly firecrackers?"

Now you're mad. "They had no right to scare me like that," you tell yourself. "I've got to get even."

Just then you notice the woman you pushed. She's trying to brush the dirt from her dress.

Choices: You chase after the boys, looking for revenge (turn to page 67).

You walk over to the woman to apologize for your behavior (turn to page 23).

You climb back down the narrow ladder. As the train climbs a steep incline, you suddenly lose your grip. Falling toward the tracks below, you reach out for something to hang on to. You grab desperately at an iron bar that protrudes from the coupling between the two last cars.

The weight of your falling pushes the bar down, and to your amazement releases the coupling. The engine and all but the last car continue up the hill and head into a tunnel. But the last car, which is now freewheeling, begins to roll back down the hill. You hold on for dear life, trying to keep your feet raised above the now flying railroad ties. Finally the railroad car slows down and comes to a stop. The door to the baggage car swings open and a clerk steps out to see what has happened. About then a horseman with gun drawn rides out from the nearby trees and forces the clerk to surrender the money bags.

"Nice work, kid," the gunman says. "I'll give you a ride down the trail."

Unable to think of any other alternative, you accept the ride. It turns out to be longer than you think. You are several days on the trail before you come to the next town. The gunman has offered to give you enough money to get a train ticket and you decide to accept. As you approach town, he stops his horse quickly.

"It's too late for you, kid," he comments.

"What you do you mean?"

"See that poster?" He points to a freshly nailed sign.

You stare in disbelief. There on the poster is an artist's sketch of the gunman—and you! Under the picture it states, "Dangerous Train Robbers Wanted: Dead or Alive!"

"Looks like we both better head for the hills," he suggests.

Stunned, you nod your head.

THE END

You clutch the top of the train. Then you spot some real trouble. Up ahead, moving your direction, is the spout of a large water tower used to replenish the train's steam engine. You have no choice but to reach out and clutch the spout; if you don't, it will knock you off the moving train.

You find yourself suspended in space as the train passes underneath you. There you are, stuck fifteen feet in the air. It's possible that you might crawl up the spout to the tower and then climb down the tower ladder. But the spout is slick, and you're not sure you can make it.

Choices: **You decide to hold on awhile and wait for someone to come along to help (turn to page 19).**
You attempt to crawl up the spout (turn to page 20).

You're spread like an eagle, clinging to the waterspout, when you notice a cloud of dust in the distance. You hope help is coming.

Soon a family in a horse-drawn wagon appears. They stop next to the tower. You speak to them, but they answer in a language you don't understand. They look Oriental, maybe Chinese. There is a man, a woman, and three children.

After what seems like an endless family discussion, the man repositions his wagon and spreads out the hay in the back of it. He grabs a rope that's tied to the spout and pulls it toward the wagon. The hinged spout swings around, and you are now hanging right above the wagon.

A girl, about your age, looks in a book. Then she points to you and announces, "Sacrifice!"

"Ah!" the whole family says together, "Sacrifice!"

Choices: You decide they want you to drop, so you let go (turn to page 21).
You fear what they have in mind for you when you get down, so you hang on (turn to page 29).

After a struggle, you do make it to the top of the tower. The tank is full of water. The only way to make it to the ladder is to swim across the tank.

The water feels cool to your hand. You pull off your shoes and socks, tie them together, and try to hold them on top of your head. You ease into the water.

It feels great. You swim over to the ladder, shove your shoes and socks in the top rung, and push out to swim around the tank a few more times. While you're at the far side, you think you hear a wagon. By the time you climb up on the edge of the tower, the wagon is long gone.

Before you leave the tank, you dive to the bottom just once, to see if you can touch it. You do hit bottom. While there, you notice a handle. When you grab hold of it, it breaks free. You come to the top holding a box.

As you hang on to the side of the tank, you realize the box is too heavy to lift out of the water. The markings on the side read: "The United States Mint/Denver."

"I'll take that, kid," a voice rings out in the silence. You turn to see a cowboy looking across the water at you from the ladder.

Turn to page 31.

As you roll in the hay, the girl comes over to talk to you. "Hello," she says.

"Hi," you answer. "Do you speak English?"

"Hello," she says again.

"I appreciate your helping me, but what did you mean by *sacrifice*? What are you going to do with me?"

"Hello," she repeats.

"Hello, hello," you mimic. "Is that all you can say?"

She shakes her head and smiles, "Hello."

The parents talk to her; she climbs up into the wagon and sits beside you. She pulls out her little book. You assumed it was a Chinese/English dictionary, but no—it's a Bible. The title page reads, "The Chinese Missionary Society, San Franciso, California." As the girl turns the pages, you notice the English words printed right alongside the Chinese.

The girl begins to point at English words. It takes quite awhile but you finally get the message. They invite you to ride to town with them. You nod your head, and they all climb in the wagon. You're headed toward Heartland.

The girl turns to the Bible, points to a whole verse, and then points to her family.

Turn to page 38.

Wham! It's like a sonic boom! Sunlight breaks into the speeding Amtrak car. The Pratts from St. Louis sit right behind you. "It's back to normal," you almost shout. You heave a deep sigh of relief. Mrs. Pratt smiles at you.

"I'm sure glad to be out of that place," you tell her.

"The tunnel?" she prompts.

"No, I mean Heartland, and all that confusion between the two tunnels. Those folks are weird. They act like it's the 1880s or something. They don't even have telephones, and . . ."

"Two tunnels?" Mr. Pratt interrupts. "We've only gone through one. See, right here on the map. It's called the Quartz Mountain Tunnel."

"Are, are you sure?" you say uncertainly. You look at the map and see that Mr. Pratt is right.

Mrs. Pratt pats her husband's arm. "Now, dear, it's just a child's adventure."

She turns back to you. "Well, you'll have plenty of wild times at Disneyland now, won't you?"

You turn around in your seat, and mumble under your breath, "I doubt it. I really doubt it."

THE END

"Ma'am, I'm really sorry. I mean, I was so scared I just panicked. Are you okay?" You try to apologize to the lady in the blue-flowered dress.

She puts her arm around you. "I understand," she says. "Anyway, all the commotion got me off at the right station. I almost slept right through it. Where are you going all by yourself?"

"California," you reply.

"Is that so? I'm going there myself. Maybe we could travel together. What city?"

"Anaheim, to see my aunt."

"What a coincidence. That's where I'm going, too. I'm a teacher. I'll be starting some Sunday schools out there. Do you go to Sunday school?"

Choices: You tell her yes (turn to page 129).
You tell her no (turn to page 28).

Inside the storeroom of the depot, you find a stack of western clothes. Several things look as though they might fit you. You try some on, just to see what they do for you, and then look in an old mirror leaning against one wall.

The jeans are almost new. The bright red shirt has fancy silver tassels along the back stitching. Even one pair of the boots fits. They have a rough, leathery, even scaly, texture. You try on the hat, too, and the gun and holster.

You're a little nervous about touching the gun. But you parade in front of the mirror and comment to yourself, "Not bad, not bad at all."

Still gazing into the mirror, you suddenly see someone at the back of the room. Startled, you swing around.

Turn to page 36.

You have a perfect view of the brawl from the balcony. A huge bearded man is swinging away at a smaller man several are calling mayor. It hardly seems fair.

A woman is nearly hysterical. She keeps yelling, "Do something! Pull them apart!" The one called mayor is getting pulverized.

You pick up a short four-by-four post and get ready to jump on the bearded man.

"Hey, kid, I wouldn't do that if I were you," a voice says. You see an arm motioning to you from behind a nearby curtained doorway.

Choices: **You jump on the big man while there's still time to save the mayor's life (turn to page 39).**
You rush to see who's warning you and why (turn to page 74).

The girl and her father drive right into the midst of the train holdup, shouting and yelling. *They'll get themselves killed!* you think. *I should have gone with them, or at least tried to stop them.*

The Chinese man puts up a good fight. Several of the would-be robbers are decked before he goes down. One of the outlaws grabs the girl.

You view it all from your hilltop lookout. The diversion gives the train crew a chance to get the rig moving, and the train starts to pull away in the midst of much yelling and shooting. The outlaws, with the captured girl, follow the train, but then they drop off and head toward the river. You, the mother, and the little children run all the way to the tracks. You motion for her to take care of her husband while you follow after the girl.

You begin to run down the road after the train robbers. You are quickly exhausted, but you

keep running. Soon your legs are aching and your lungs are struggling to get another breath. There is a sharp pain in your side; still you just keep plugging along. Finally you can go no farther. You stop to rest under a tree just off the path.

As you lie flat on a huge pine log, you hear voices just over the granite boulders to the north.

"It's the outlaws!" you silently exclaim. "I almost ran into them."

"Let's trade her to the Indians. She's no good to us. We can't even understand a word she says," a deep voice suggests. Others agree. You know that you must do something soon, but you are so tired. Just then a fierce voice shouts, "Hey, there's a kid over here!"

You've been discovered!

Turn to page 133.

"No, Ma'am," you admit, "not too often."

"I'm holding a Bible school right here in Heartland tonight and tomorrow morning. How about joining us at the Grange Hall? You never have to travel alone when the Lord is beside you."

"Oh, sure—if I'm still around," you tell her.

The lady smiles and hikes down the street carrying a large satchel and a small brown bag.

"Hey!" a man at the station calls out to you. "Are you the Chicago Kid?"

"Yeah," you reply, thinking that he means "Are you from Chicago?" You rush over, hoping he has your ticket to California.

"You look younger than I expected, Kid," he greets you. "But you do look sorta like your picture. Lefty arrived this morning and brought your gear. It's over in the storeroom. You can dress there, if you like. I bet you're anxious to get out of those city clothes. Gee, Kid, no offense, but those are sure funny-looking shoes."

You look down at your tennis shoes, and then back at the agent. "I'm afraid you've confused me with someone else," you explain.

"Don't worry, Kid, not a soul knows you're in town," he assures you. "Now go on, get your gear."

Choices: You reply, "I've got to get to California—fast" (turn to page 30).
You go to the storeroom to see what's there (turn to page 24).

"No sacrifice, no sacrifice!" you shout back at them.

After much discussion, they turn to one of the younger children and say something. He produces a slingshot and searches around for a rock.

"They're going to shoot me!" you think to yourself. A sharp pain stabs you in the seat of the pants. You let go of the waterspout and fall down into the soft hay below.

"Well, I'm down," you moan. "Now what?"

Turn to page 21.

"Well, I'll be," the man replies. "Maybe Byron and the boys were right. They said you'd be afraid to show up at the rodeo."

"What?" you sputter.

"They figured your winning the suicide race last year was a fluke. Why, they've even raised the purse just to lure you back. I guess you're going to pretend you don't know anything about that, either."

"I told you," you protest. "You've got the wrong . . ."

"Yeah, I heard. If that's your game, go ahead and play it. But I wouldn't enter Tough Town without your gear. See you later, Kid. And don't try running off to California," he warns. Then he adds, "I'd advise you to go see Lefty before you do something you'll regret. He's over at the Nugget."

You walk down the street, hoping to find something to eat. You stop at a place called Madame Peer's Emporium. A clerk with sinister eyes informs you that this is a clothing store, not a cafe. As you leave, a tall lady in a long black dress enters from a back room and says, "There you are! I've been expecting you. Come on back here."

Choices: You say, "No, thanks," and run out (turn to page 37).
You follow the lady into the back room (turn to page 35).

"Who are you?" you ask nervously.

"Big Curly Oliver," he replies. "And your name will be mud if you don't give me that box." He spits something out of his mouth and continues, "I'll make you a trade. You bring the box over here, and I won't throw your shoes out into the canyon."

Choices: You drop the box back into the water and say, "Get it yourself" (turn to page 68).
You work your way around the edge and hand the box to the man (turn to page 55).

Just as you hop on the horse, it gets spooked by the crowd. The horse bolts down the street while you hang on as best you can. You hear a woman screech, "Stop that kid! Horse thief!"

You couldn't stop the horse if you wanted to. Half an hour later, and who knows how many miles from town, the horse pauses to drink at a creek. You dismount and scoop up some water, too.

"I like the way you ride, kid." A man leads a horse toward you from a grove of cottonwood trees. His spurs jingle as he walks.

"That your horse?" he asks.

"No," you answer. "I was just sitting on it, and it got frightened and sort of ran this way."

"I see. . . . How'd you like to earn some money helping me push a herd of cattle up to Canada?"

"Thanks, but I'm on my way to California."

"It takes silver and gold out there. It's the only thing they use. Look, kid, let's be honest. You rode out of town on somebody else's horse. That's stealing. You'll be strung up before the parade starts. Or, you can go to Canada with me. We'll sell the cattle to the miners and make a bundle. Then you can go to California in style."

Turn to page 94.

As you finish praying, the buffalo spies the opening at the top of the crate. He must have had sudden thoughts of freedom. He kicks down the back of the crate and escapes. You hide behind some luggage, since he looks as though he's going wild after his confinement.

The whole baggage car is almost torn apart. The conductor opens the door to see what the commotion is, and the buffalo charges him. The hefty railroad man leaps back to safety, and the buffalo storms into the passenger car. People run and scramble everywhere.

During the commotion you slip out the door without being noticed. There are two things you need at once: to call your dad and to get something to eat. But you're shocked to find that this strange town has no phones and no McDonald's. A crazy sign straddles the main street: 4th of July, 1885 Parade. *They even misprinted their sign,* you think.

An idea flits through your mind: *What if it isn't a misprint?* But you shake the thought off as ridiculous and continue your search for some lunch.

Choices: **If you like Chinese food, you go to the Hong Kong Noodle Company Cafe (turn to page 72).**
If you don't like Chinese food, you enter Marshall's Meat Menagerie (turn to page 93).

The back room is very nice. It's furnished with brown leather chairs and has tan velvet wallpaper. The lady sits down and offers you a sandwich. You accept. She wants to know all about you. You're not sure if you should trust her, but she's the first person who's listened to you, so you tell all.

"I understand completely," she replies.

"You do?" you respond. "Even the part about being from a different century?"

"Of course," she says with a smile. "I'm not from this time, either."

You feel a shiver up your back. "You're not? Where are you from?"

She laughs. "Now, you can't expect a woman to reveal her age, can you?"

You relax a little and laugh with her.

"Come here," she coaxes. "I want you to try something." She hands you a hoop. "Can you slip this over you?"

You pass the hoop over your head and body with ease.

"Very good," she almost purrs. "Now, I've got something special to show you."

Turn to page 44.

It's an old man. He's wearing blue coveralls and a faded red flannel undershirt. He grins and scratches his head. "Heh, heh. You the Chicago Kid?" he asks.

"What if I am?" you reply defensively.

"Jest askin', Kid. Jest askin'. I ain't never seen no famous cowhand like you close up, that's all," he says.

Just then the heavy gun belt starts to slip off your hip. You reach down to pull up your belt, but by accident grab the gun handle instead. You stand there with a drawn gun.

"Don't shoot, Kid. Don't shoot. I don't mean you no harm. I'm just a mouthy old man. I'm a'leavin'. I'm a'leavin'." The man rushes out the back door and down the alley.

Choices: You take off the gun and holster and leave them in the storeroom (turn to page 66).

You take all the bullets out of the gun and continue to wear it (turn to page 89).

You wear the gun with the bullets still in it (turn to page 54).

You hurry toward the door. But the unpleasant-looking employee blocks the doorway. He's also holding a foot-long knitting needle.

Choices: **You decide you might as well stay a while (turn to page 35).**
You shove a bolt of cloth through the glass window and dive headfirst onto the wooden sidewalk outside (turn to page 128).

The verse that the girl points to is Romans 10:9, "If thou shalt confess with thy mouth the Lord Jesus, and shalt believe in thine heart that God hath raised him from the dead, thou shalt be saved."

A few more rounds of picking out words confirms to you that this family is Christian. By the time you've traveled several miles, it's occurred to you what they meant by "sacrifice." To them, it meant to let go of your life. They wanted to encourage you to drop down into the hay.

You point to the title page and say, "California."

You discover that they're headed to San Francisco right now. When you reach Heartland, they invite you to accompany them.

Choices: **You politely decline and head for the Heartland train depot** **(turn to page 43).**

You accept their offer **(turn to page 46).**

You fly off the balcony and crash right on top of the bearded man's head. With all your might, you swing out with the four-by-four post.

Choices: **If you weigh more than 100 pounds, (turn to page 75).**
If you weigh less than 100 pounds, (turn to page 52).

You wake up staring into the eyes of the buffalo. Your head hurts like crazy. Besides that, your right ankle smarts when you try to walk.

Hobbling along, you try to chase the little buffalo into the surrounding mountains, but each time he wanders back to you. You cross the tracks toward town. You figure you might need some medical care. The buffalo, whom you've nicknamed "Bullet," tags along.

As you limp into town, a well-dressed man on horseback hollers at you, "Hey, is that your buffalo?"

"No, sir. It's just following me. I can't seem to get rid of it."

"Well, that's quite a show. Let me introduce myself. I'm J. T. Russell, of Russell's Roundup Rodeo. We could use an act like that during the breaks. Would you be interested in joining the show this afternoon? There's ten dollars in it for you. We'll even feed the buffalo."

"I don't know," you answer uncertainly. "I've got to get ahold of my dad."

"Sure, kid, where is he?"

"Chicago."

"You've got to be kidding," the man responds with surprise.

Turn to page 47.

"It's that kid!" the conductor shouts. He and another man pull you out of the barrel. "Brett, report this to the sheriff. Maybe he'll know what to do."

Brett drags you down the street by your arm. "Look," you protest, "I'm on my way to California to visit my aunt. She'll be worried if I'm not on that train. Call her up and ask her yourself."

"Do what?"

"Call her on the phone," you repeat. "I know her number."

Brett stops and pulls your face close to his. "What are you talking about? What's a phone?"

You begin to have a sinking feeling. "Where am I anyway?"

"This is Heartland, Montana Territory."

Territory? "What's the date?" you inquire.

"July 4th, 1885. Now, stop your stalling." He pushes you into the sheriff's office. "A runaway, Sheriff, and a little touched at that."

"Well, kid, let's have your story," the sheriff demands.

Choices: You tell him the truth about the tunnel and all (turn to page 53).

You make up a story that you hope will get you back on the train (turn to page 59).

The counter at the train depot posts a small sign reading, "Closed for Lunch." You sit down on a bench and wait for someone to return. In the meantime, you make friends with a dog who's snooping around the station. At one point, the dog yanks with his teeth a bright green duffel bag that had been leaning against the bench.

The playful dog hauls the bag down onto the railroad tracks. You worry about it staying there. But when you try to retrieve it, the dog drags it farther down the tracks.

Finally, you dive for it and wrestle it away from the dog. Just then someone at the station yells out, "Stop that kid. That's my luggage that's been stolen!"

Choices: You drop the bag and run down the tracks away from the station (turn to page 70).
You return to the station platform with the bag (turn to page 51).

You stare at a detailed, three-dimensional scale model of a small city and surrounding countryside. "Wow, it looks like a miniature town," you exclaim.

"It is. It's Heartland. And we're standing right here," she says, pointing. "All those tubes represent tunnels under the city. They're part of the Colonel Brown Silver Mine. Some of the shafts are not bigger than that hoop."

She stops and leans closer to you. "Now, here's my plan. I don't want to stay in this century any more than you do. The mountain tunnel contains a historical time warp. It has to be broken. I figure with the right amount of explosives, I can blow up the tunnel. It'll destroy the warp, and we'll end up back in your century."

"But that could blow up the whole town, couldn't it?" you suggest.

"Perhaps, perhaps not. The important thing is, we'd be restoring the balance of history. It's got to be done, or the planet will eventually blow apart due to its antiquitous lopsidedness. You do understand, don't you?"

"But, you can't . . . ," you try to say.

"Sure we can," she grins.

We?" you interject. "What do you mean *we?*"

Turn to page 56

You thank the woman. As you walk along with her, you ask her name.

"You can call me Aunt Julie, like everyone else does," she said. "Now, did I hear right, you ain't got no kin around these parts?"

"I'm traveling to go see *my* Aunt Julie in California. They told me I had to get off here."

"Well," she said. "You just can't trust folks. You crawl under those tarps in the back of the wagon until we get out of town. If they wanted you here that bad, they won't let you get out without a ruckus."

You crawl under the tarp. Then something heavy is thrown on top of you. You can't move an inch. You can't even cry out. Then you hear the woman talking to someone.

"Come on, Paul. Let's get going before we're seen. This one ain't too bad. A bit daft is all. I figure this one could last two, maybe three months down in the mine."

The one named Paul roars. "Yeah, and staying under that tarp will get 'em used to the dark. It'll be a long, long time 'til that young'un sees daylight again."

THE END

You travel slowly most of the afternoon. As the wagon crests a steep hill, the father excitedly points down into the valley. In the distance you can all see a train stopped. All the passengers are lined up along the west side. "Someone's robbing the train," you blurt out.

The family chatters among itself and then stops as the girl turns to you. "Father . . . must . . . stop," she explains, pointing to certain words.

The mother and smaller children are let out by a large tree. The man motions to you to do the same.

Choices: **You get out and find a good viewing spot from the hilltop (turn to page 26). You insist on going with the girl and her father (turn to page 69).**

"That's two thousand miles away. It would probably take two days even to get a telegram through from here. . . . What are you doing out west all by yourself, anyway?"

Before you can respond, a lady rushes up to you. "I'm Mrs. Edgars, owner of the *Heartland Gazette.* Could we get a story and picture of you and the pet buffalo for the paper? It would make a great cover story."

"Sure, I guess so," you reply.

"Good. I'm on my way to a meeting at the bank. Could you meet me right here at one o'clock? Be sure and bring the buffalo."

"But I just promised Mr. Russell here I'd be in his rodeo at one o'clock."

"Well, if I'm going to make it into tomorrow's edition, I can't wait any later than that. What's it going to be?"

Choices: You decide to have your story and picture in the newspaper (turn to page 91).

You enter the rodeo (turn to page 136).

As you cross the street toward the bank, a man rushes out of the Silver Dollar Hotel and hollers, "Hey, kid, run get Doc Haney. Mr. Way is choking to death!"

He quickly disappears back into the hotel. You hesitate. You have no idea where Doc Haney is. And no one's in sight at the moment.

You take a peek inside the hotel. A man in a black suit is lying on the floor, gasping for breath. Several adults stand around doing nothing.

The man who hollered at you sees you and screams, "Don't just stand there, get the doc!"

Choices: You run down the street screaming, "Doc Haney! Doc Haney!" (turn to page 142).

You scoot over to the stricken man, grab him from behind, and jam your clenched fists into his stomach as hard as you can (turn to page 96).

Your hands barely catch the rear rail of the wagon. It starts to drag you along. The two men don't know you're back there.

Choices: If you can chin yourself three times, turn to page 87.
If you can't chin yourself three times, turn to page 64.

It's dark in the room. As soon as you enter, you hear a lock catch behind you. "Oh, no," you moan. "I ran right into the closet they were talking about."

For several hours you feel your way around by searching the walls and along the floor. One area of the wooden floor feels colder than the rest. You take a nickel out of your pocket and drop it through a crack in the wood. A couple seconds later it hits something hard that sounds like cement.

You wonder if you might be able to escape under the building if you dig through the flooring.

The door swings open. The unexpected light blinds you. "Here," Madame Peer's assistant grunts. "You'd better eat something."

The door slams shut. You grope through the darkness for the plate of food. You're not hungry, but you're delighted to find a spoon and fork. Soon you're busy chipping away at the floorboards. But you seem to be getting nowhere.

Choices: You give up, and try to think of another way to escape (turn to page 65).

You're determined to keep at it as long as it takes (turn to page 81).

Rapidly you explain about the dog. "I was only trying to get the bag back for you."

He seems satisfied when he examines the contents. It's full of masks.

"What are those for?" you ask.

"I'm an actor. These are some of my props. I'll be doing a show at the Heartland Follies this afternoon right after the rodeo. Have you seen a kid in a blue cutoff suit? He's my partner."

"No, afraid not," you reply.

"He was supposed to be on this train. If he missed it, I'm sunk." He sits down in a heap on the bench. "Say, I don't suppose you've done any acting? You're about his size."

"Who, me? Well, I was Scrooge in the Christmas play," you inform him.

His face brightens. "In four hours you could be center stage with hundreds of cheering fans. What do you say—will you help me out?"

Just then you see the man return to the ticket window.

"Come on," prompts the actor. "Do you want to be famous or not?"

Choices: You decide to be in the play (turn to page 135).

You turn him down and try to get a ticket for California (turn to page 116).

Even though you score a direct hit, the huge man barely seems fazed. He turns, grabs you by the shirt, and throws you halfway across the street. You land headfirst in a horse trough.

You feel a strong hand pushing your head under the water. "Lord," you pray as your lungs are about to burst, "Get me out of this, quick! Please!"

Just then you're released. You gasp for air. Your attacker is hopping around the street holding his foot. A young girl, holding a heavy blacksmith's hammer, calls for you to follow her. As you follow her through the crowd, she states the obvious, "I hit him on the toe with this."

She leads you to a stack of boards next to a hen house. "You can hide here till it's over."

"Hey, thanks for saving me back there. I was down to my last prayer."

"Oh," she says with curiosity, "what were you praying?"

"You know, asking God to get me out of that mess."

"Do you really think he heard you?" she quizzes.

"Sure," you reply. "Where are you going?"

"I've got to help my dad. No one else will."

Choices: You wait behind the hen house (turn to page 76).

You go with the girl (turn to page 78).

You finish your tale as the sheriff listens patiently. He actually seems to understand. "Well, kid, I think I know just the folks who can help you."

"You do?" you ask, genuinely surprised.

"Let me go make some arrangements first," he says as he leaves you in the office.

You stare at the posters on the walls. After you've read them all, you decide the meanest outlaw is a man called Mountain Mike. Then the sheriff returns.

"It's all set. You needn't worry about a thing. But, you will have to spend a night in my cell, just to keep you off the streets. I wouldn't want you getting yourself hurt. In the morning, I'll put you on a stage to Bozeman. Show the attendants there this paper."

You look at the scrap of official paper that says "Rocky Mountain Sanitarium."

They're sending me to an asylum! you realize.

Choices: You grab a cup of coffee from the desk and throw it at the sheriff as you break for the door (turn to page 57).

You don't know what to do, so you follow the sheriff to the jail cell (turn to page 58).

When you've walked about fifty feet down the street, a little boy yells out, "The Chicago Kid's coming! And the Kid's wearing guns!"

You walk another block, and someone from the top of the Heartland Hotel shouts down at you. He's holding a rifle, pointed straight at you. "Kid, you aren't going to the race today!" he announces.

Choices: You say, "Sure, that's fine. Be glad to oblige you, sir" (turn to page 113).
You grab your pistol and fire wildly toward the top of the hotel (turn to page 114).

"You're a smart kid," he says, "but not smart enough." He tosses your shoes as far as he can throw them in separate directions.

"But you promised to give me my shoes," you remind him.

"Wrong. I promised not to throw them in the canyon. See you around." He starts down the ladder with the heavy box.

Choices: You follow after the cowboy with red in your eye (turn to page 83).
You stay where you are and slowly count to fifty (turn to page 132).

"I need your help in the tunnel to set the explosives," Madame Peer continues.

"I won't do it," you say without hesitation.

"Of course you will. It's your only hope of getting back to the twentieth century."

"I still won't do it," you insist.

"We'll see, we'll see," she says quietly. "Ruckman," she calls to the creepy-looking clerk, "lock the kid in the closet. You know which one."

Choices: To gain more time to think, you tell Madame Peer you'll work with her (turn to page 85).
You shout, "What's that behind you?" and run through the back door (turn to page 50).

You stumble across the wooden plank side-walk, trip and fall in the dust, and stagger to your feet.

"Come on, kid." A cowboy on a buckskin horse offers you his arm. Soon you're riding behind him, hurrying out of town. "I know a trail they'll never find," he shouts back to you.

The horse leaves the dirt trail and ascends a very steep rock cliff. You close your eyes most of the way up and hang on tight. You sigh with deep relief when you finally stop and spy the town of Heartland hundreds of feet below you. "It looks so different from up here," you muse softly as the two of you dismount.

The tall man whacks his hat against his leg several times. "So, what's the sheriff want you for?" he asks.

"Nothing. That's just it, I didn't do anything . . ." You're not very eager to tell him your story, so you hesitate.

"Yeah, I know what you mean . . ." The cowboy reaches into his saddlebag and pulls out several pieces of dried meat. "Have a bite of elk. You'll need the strength."

The tough jerky tastes spicy and good. You listen quietly as he continues. "Seems to me you've got several options from here."

Turn to page 80.

The tiny jail cell about suffocates you. You stay awake most of the night trying to figure out what to do next. Between prayers and tears you get pretty hungry. In the morning, the sheriff brings you a plate of biscuits and gravy for breakfast.

"Can I talk to a minister before you send me away?" you inquire.

"Not hardly," the sheriff informs you. "We don't see no preachers around these parts more than once a month. Now, you just come along nice and peaceful, and we won't tie you up."

You ride in a wagon heading north. There's just one other passenger besides you and the driver. He's an older man, and has both his hands and feet tied. During the long day you tell the man your whole situation. He's fascinated and pumps you for details. When you finish, he leans close to you and whispers, "Do you have any idea who you're talking to?"

"No, I don't. Who are you?"

"My name's George Washington. I'm the father of this here country, and look how they're treating me."

You look the man's face over carefully before it dawns on you. You could spend the rest of your life locked up with people like him. The first moment you feel brave enough, you leap from the speeding wagon.

Turn to page 122.

"My dad's got a big ranch west of here," you lie. "It's called the Ponderosa. And I've got three brothers named Adam, Hoss, and Little Joe. I was kidnapped by a bunch of no-good drifters and barely got loose."

"I thought you were on the train to visit your aunt," the sheriff said. "Just how far west is your father's ranch?"

"Oh, I guess about a hundred miles."

"That's strange. I've never heard of it. Well, you get out of here. But if I find you around town tonight, I'll have to do something about it." The lawman points you to the door.

"Yes, sir."

"And if I were you, I'd enter the pie-eating contest down at the school yard. First prize is a new pair of boots. From the looks of things, you could use something decent on your feet."

"But these are tennis shoes . . ." you start to say, and then you rush quickly out the door.

Choices: You head for the school grounds to enter the pie-eating contest (turn to page 60).

You head back across town to try to find the train depot (turn to page 9).

At the school yard, about twenty-five kids sit at a long table in front of a line of berry pies. There's just one empty place. You rush to it just as someone raises a gun. It fires and everyone dives into the pies. Yours tastes so good you gulp it right down.

By the time you reach for your fifth pie, you realize a number of people are cheering you on. Most of the other contestants are holding their stomachs or are stretched out on the grass. You finish your last bite and stand, stains and all. A man with a string tie and straw hat awards you a certificate and pair of boots.

"What kind of berries were those?" you ask him a little later. You're beginning to feel a little queasy.

"Huckleberry," answers the man with a heavy Swedish accent.

"Huckleberry! You mean there really is such a thing? I thought that was just something made

up for the cartoons."

"The what?"

"Never mind. Say, I know how you can make even better pies," you suggest.

"You know about baking? I thought I was the only baker in town."

"You take some very cold cream, beat it hard until it whips up, and then serve it fresh on top of the berries. Mmmmm, is it good."

You go with the man to his shop and demonstrate the process.

"How about going into business with me," he offers. "We could make some money on this."

The next morning you wake up in back of the bakery to the sounds of hammering. Your partner hangs up a new sign, "Johansson & Kid Bakery." You should have the money to go on to California very soon.

THE END

You hide in the brush, escaping the notice of the two men, who stop to pick up the broken barrel pieces. They seem to be looking for something—the black box, you suppose.

After a long search, they jump back into the wagon and drive away. You investigate the box. Carefully packed in shredded paper are two jars marked #1 and #2. There's a danger sign attached. One of the liquids is a thick, light yellow substance. The other is clear. You cradle the box under your arm and walk in the direction of town.

It's a hot day. You're soon sweaty and thirsty. The thought crosses your mind to drink the liquids, but they smell horrible. You get tired of carrying them, so you throw the yellow one as far as you can. It crashes against the granite cliff. Then you heave the second one. Just as it touches the rocks there's a terrific explosion. You're thrown to the ground.

"It was some kind of explosive," you moan as you drag yourself up and shake the dirt out of your hair and ears. You decide to investigate a little closer, and find that a crater has been formed where the liquids landed. It's beginning to fill up with a sticky black substance.

You climb down inside to touch and smell the dark stuff. "It's oil!" you exclaim. "I've discovered oil!" You look up and are startled to see several men on horseback perched on the rim. They don't look very happy.

"Did you do this, kid?" one of them asks.

"It was an accident. But look at all this oil!"

"Yes, we know. That's what ruins the drinking water around here. Makes the land useless."

"Useless! What about fuel for your trains?"

"Fuel for trains? Every fool knows trains run on steam made by burning wood. That stuff doesn't even make good axle grease. The whole country's worthless, even for cattle. Don't be exploding any more dynamite and messing up the range, you hear?"

You nod, and the men leave. You do a lot of thinking as you continue to town. It's 1885. In twenty years there'll be cars. That means a need for oil. This property could be worth millions. In twenty years, you'll be thirty-two years old. You could be a billionaire before you're forty! If this is open range, you can file a claim and homestead it.

You reach town and find the claims office. "You find gold?" the man behind the desk inquires.

"Something even better," you reply. "Something even better."

THE END

You find yourself tumbling to the road. As you lie in the loose soil, you watch the wagon crest a hill. You decide to forget the wagon and the box and return to town.

Turn to page 13.

You spend the next hour close to tears as you look for a way out. You decide to keep chipping away at the floorboards with your spoon. Just as you dig through the first board, the door opens and Madame Peer's assistant grabs you by the back of the neck. "Trying to get away, huh? Fat chance of that. That old silver mine tunnel under there would have been your grave. There are so many cross turns you'd never find your way out."

He ties you up and loads you onto a wagon. Hours later you, the assistant, and Madame Peer arrive at a ranch. They throw you on a cot in the corner of a living room. You're in a big ranch house of some kind. Your two companions seem to be waiting for someone. Several men arrive, and you overhear their plot. They're going to blow up the tunnels, with your help.

In all the talking, you hear them mention some soldiers on the other side of the granite mountains. That gets you busier than ever trying to untie yourself. The long ride in the wagon seems to have loosened the ropes a bit. As soon as you're free, you race out the front door and jump on the nearest saddled horse. You hope it's a fast one.

Turn to page 109.

The western clothes fit okay. They certainly blend in with what everyone else is wearing. But people keep staring at you as you walk down the street. You hear one of them mumble, "The Chicago Kid? without guns?"

A man with a bandaged arm and black eye meets you. "Kid! Welcome to Heartland. I'm Mayor Ward. I want you to know we're glad you've accepted the position as Territorial Governor. We had our doubts you'd take the job, but we remember what you said."

"What?" you say in bewilderment.

"You told us when you left for the capital that if you returned without your guns, that meant you'd do it. If you didn't come back at all, that meant they hung you," the mayor concludes with a nervous smile.

Then he lowers his voice. "Of course, things are complicated around here with Mountain Mike in town. But I'm sure you can handle him, right? There's a big reception going on over at the Grange Hall. Let's make the announcement."

Thundering applause greets you at the Grange Hall. You ache from all the slaps on the back. A woman offers you a deluxe suite at the Palace Hotel for your office and living quarters. You thank her. It's nice having everyone call you Governor. Then a man bulging with muscles bursts through the hotel lobby. As you stare, someone near you gasps, "It's Mountain Mike! He must be looking for the Kid!"

Turn to page 77.

You follow the two boys, keeping your distance in the shadows. When they sit down on a bench in front of the general store, you sneak around the back. Behind the building is a small wooden shack with foreign writing on one side. The writing looks Chinese. The shack is locked, but some boards hang loose. You pull some of them apart and crawl inside. The whole room is stacked high with fireworks.

You grab several round tubes that look like huge firecrackers and tie them together with wire that's lying on the floor. You're surprised to discover a box of matches on a nearby table. You creep out of the shack with the biggest firecracker you've ever seen.

The boys are watching a fistfight across the street. They don't notice as you slip up behind them. You place your firecracker near the bench and light the fuse. Then you scurry around the corner to watch.

Turn to page 130.

He doesn't look pleased. "You shouldn't have done that," he says. He slips out his gun. "See that pinecone on top of that tallest tree?"

You barely have time to focus your eyes before he fires a shot. Before the cone drops ten feet, a second shot rips the air. The cone shatters to the ground.

"Now, I ain't never shot a kid before," he announces as he spits. "But you just might be the first."

You dive for the box and hand it to the cowboy.

Turn to page 55.

The man and the girl allow you to join them. The three of you storm right in to the holdup. You try to get the man to slip up from the south side. He doesn't understand you. Instead, he flies off the wagon and lands on one of the outlaws; then he jumps to his feet and knocks down another.

You and the girl tackle a third man. There's mass confusion. The train begins to pull away and you hear shots close by. The Chinese man is hit. He falls to the ground, and the girl runs to him. You feel a sharp blow to your head.

When you regain consciousness, you and the girl are tied to the railroad tracks. You look at the girl. She smiles back and says, "Jesus saves."

"Yeah, yeah," you mumble, "but I hoped heaven would wait a few more years."

She just smiles again and repeats the words, "Jesus saves."

The rails rumble beneath you. The track vibrates violently. "A train!" you scream in panic. In a wild frenzy, you attempt to yank yourself free.

"Jesus saves," the girl exclaims with rising excitement.

In utter terror you wrench your body in every direction. Then, as the train roars nearer, you faint.

Turn to page 134.

On the outskirts of town, you peer around to see if anyone's following. No one is. So you circle around and sneak back toward the depot.

As you pass a school yard, you notice flags and banners everywhere. One banner reads, "Twelfth Annual Heartland Pie-Eating Contest." Suddenly you're very, very hungry.

Turn to page 60.

You don't hear any noise.

Your bones aren't crushed.

Everything's perfectly still.

Cautiously you open one eye, then the other.

The young buffalo sits quietly beside you. He's staring out the open baggage car door. You slip out of the car as quickly as you can while the animal continues to gaze out in space.

Heartland surprises you. It's like a scene out of a western movie. There are stagecoaches, unpaved streets, and men wearing guns. The train itself is no longer the sleek Amtrak you boarded in Chicago. It's an old steam-powered rig with ancient-looking passenger cars.

Everything is happening too fast. You sit down and rub your head.

"You aren't getting off this train!" a male voice booms from somewhere nearby.

You jerk to attention and crane to see what the commotion is. The sight that greets you raises goose bumps all over your body.

Turn to page 92.

You sit down at a table in the dimly lit room. A woman wearing a colorful silk gown points you to a handwritten menu on a chalkboard above a row of glasses. You can't decipher any of the items, so you just point to several. She nods and goes into the kitchen.

You notice that most of the other patrons are Chinese. You check your wallet to see if you have enough money to pay for the food. You just have some change and several traveler's checks, but you aren't worried. You remember the TV commericals that boast these traveler's checks are good anywhere in the world.

But where in the world am I? you wonder.

The waitress displays three heaping plates of food before you. None of the dishes looks familiar, but you don't want to show your ignorance. After a plate of squishy little breaded things, you tackle the soup.

It's not too bad. You gulp the whole thing down, and then look up in astonishment as everyone in the place applauds. The waitress answers your puzzled look.

"We've never seen anyone who isn't Chinese eat a whole bowl of bird's nest soup."

"Bird's nest soup?" you repeat slowly. "What's it made of?"

"Birds' nests, of course," she replies with a bright smile.

You dash for the front door in hopes you'll make it outside before you lose that soup. You don't.

It's night before you feel like walking around town. You jump on a train just as it's pulling out, and find a place to lie down. Suddenly it's very dark. The train has entered a tunnel.

Turn to page 22.

The hand motioning to you belongs to a pretty lady dressed in black. She comes out on the balcony.

"I'm Madame Peer, and I can help you."

"You can?" You hope she's right.

"Follow me," she beckons.

You trail after her, down some outside stairs and across several alleyways. You pass some horses and chickens and a milk cow tied to a tree. Finally you enter a building that says "Madame Peer's Emporium" above the door. A creepy-looking clerk greets you. Madame Peer leads you into a back room.

Turn to page 35.

The big man tumbles to the dirt.

"You did it!" a girl screams.

"Hooray for the Kid!" cheers the crowd.

The mayor shakes himself off and soaks his wounded hand in a water trough. "You're sent from heaven, Kid," he tells you. "That was Mean Mountain Mike you just flattened. There'll be a reward in it for you."

"Reward? You mean *money*? Is it enough to buy a ticket to California?"

"Sure, and some left over for a meal or two, I reckon," the mayor announces.

He invites you to ride with him and his family as they lead the Fourth-of-July parade. You accept, and also join them at the picnic. That evening there's a fireworks show. Everyone treats you like a hero.

Just before bedtime the sheriff takes you aside. "Listen, Kid, I know you want to leave town. Sorry to hear that, 'cause I sure could use a deputy like you. I'll be retiring next winter, and you could be the next sheriff of Heartland. What do you say?"

Choices: You tell him no way—you want to go as soon as you can (turn to page 120).
You decide everything's so crazy anyway, you've got nothing to lose; you'll be his deputy (turn to page 119).

You stare as the girl turns the corner of the building and disappears from sight.

"I don't even know what I'm doing here. . . ." you moan to yourself. "All I want is to be on a train traveling to California. How come I got stuck in this stupid century?"

You stop as you suddenly realize something. That girl helped you when you were in trouble, and then you just let her go. Some Christian witness you are! You tear out from behind the chicken house and catch up with her several blocks later.

Turn to page 78.

You realize you could never beat this monster in a fight. You contemplate a tactic you once saw on a TV show.

You walk straight up to Mean Mountain Mike and say, "You've got ten minutes to get out of town. If at the end of that time you're still around, I'll be forced to use the full power of my position to bring you to justice. If, when I'm through with you, there's anything left, Judge Roy will have you hung. Do I make myself clear?"

You turn your back on him and walk toward the door. You expect either a shot in the back or a slug over the head. But nothing happens. You walk out to the front porch, where a crowd has gathered. You lean on a post in order to look relaxed. Actually, you're so scared you'd fall down if you didn't have some support.

The mayor is the first to speak. "Mean Mountain Mike just slipped out of town the back way! You did it! You chased him off without a fight!"

"I did?" you stutter. "I mean, of course I did!"

Turn to page 146.

As the two of you approach the crowd once more, you can see that the big man and the girl's father have resumed their battle. "Let's climb up here," she suggests, pointing to a stagecoach.

You can see all the action from up there. "Why is he fighting your father?" you ask the girl.

"Because he's Mean Mountain Mike, that's why. And my dad's the mayor."

You watch the girl climb down and unhook the reins of the rig.

"If Mean Mike wins, there won't be anyone left to stop him from running the town."

"What about the sheriff?"

"The sheriff's too new in town. He doesn't know which end is up yet." She now holds the reins and sits in the driver's seat.

"What are you going to do? Run over him?" you shout.

"Precisely!" she calls back.

You grab your seat as the stagecoach lurches ahead.

Turn to page 82.

The cowboy climbs back on his horse. "You can either hike across Crater Mountain to the railroad tracks, or you can ride on with me to Stone Mountain Fort. You might catch a train that slows at the tunnel on the Crater."

"Did you say *fort*? You mean, with an army and all that . . . ?"

"Ha! Not hardly! I mean like with bank robbers, horse thieves, and cutthroats. You were running from the law—well, so am I. Me and the boys have a little stone house high up in the Rockies. We can always use an extra hand around the place. And you'd enjoy meeting Butch and Sundance."

"You mean *the* Butch Cassidy?" you stammer.

"Sure. Now, what'll it be?"

Choices: You head cross-country to the train tracks (turn to page 84).
You decide to get a firsthand view of these famous outlaws (turn to page 101).

You finally break through one board, then another. Soon you've pulled up enough to climb through the old floor. You let yourself down and hit hard rock. It's a small tunnel of some sort. You feel your way along until you hear a noise behind you. In the distance you hear someone calling, "Hey, come back. Don't go in there; you'll never get out. . . ."

You can't hear what else they say as you crawl faster in the dark. You soon realize that there are many side tunnels that branch off the main one. You begin to panic. You're lost. You might even be going around in circles.

You find a tunnel that's tall enough to walk through. You stumble, fall, get up, and run. You shout and cry for help. You trip over some timber and fall again. But what a shock! You don't hit ground—you just keep falling in space.

I'm going down a vertical shaft! your mind screams.

Pitch black all around and falling, falling . . .

Surely this is all a dream and you'll soon wake up.

THE END

"Can you throw a loop?" she yells above the hoofbeats of galloping horses.

"Are you kidding?" you respond. You stare at her as if she had asked you to fly.

"Well, you'll just have to drive, then." She hands you the reins and grabs a rope. "I hope I don't catch him by the neck," she hollers. "I don't want us to get thrown in jail for killing a man."

"Lord, please, not around the neck," you pray as you clutch the reins.

You slap the reins and hope the horses gallop straight ahead. All the crowd, except the two fighters, dive for safety. The stagecoach heads straight for the two men. You have no idea how to get the thing to go to one side or the other.

"We're going to kill them both!" you holler to the girl.

Turn to page 97.

After two hundred yards your feet are raw. You decide to go back and find your shoes. Gingerly you crawl down the canyon wall where you think one shoe went over—in spite of the cowboy's "promise." That's when you see it.

A wagon has crashed over the edge of the roadway. It wasn't visible until you climbed over the boulders. As you approach, you discover an unconscious man pinned under the rig. Next to him is a leather pouch with some gold coins spilling out. The man seems dead.

Choices: **You take the coins and continue looking for your shoes (turn to page 115). You pull off the man's shoes, fit them on your own feet, and head down the road looking for help (turn to page 90).**

Crater Mountain stands taller and steeper than you first imagined. The sun is hot, and you're worn out when you reach the top. Below, you spy the train tracks as they wander across the prairie. You can even see the tunnel opening.

You can't spot any trains coming yet, but you know there'll be one sooner or later.

Choices: **You rest a few moments on top of some rocks (turn to page 100).**

In spite of near exhaustion, you hike down toward the train tracks (turn to page 86).

"Okay," you concede. "I'll do it. But I want to make sure no one will get hurt."

The lady beams at her assistant. "Of course no one will be hurt. Will they, Ruckman?"

Her henchman grins from ear to ear. You doubt their sincerity, even though they barrage you with talk about how you're helping humanity and history by destroying this freak of nature. After a while, you're almost convinced. Maybe this is an important mission, after all.

"Maybe that's why God sent me here," you say to Madame Peer.

She seems shocked. "*God* sent you here?"

"Well, not specifically, perhaps. It was just a figure of speech, sort of . . ."

She regains her composure, and her sickly sweet smile returns.

You, Madame Peer, and Ruckman ride out of town in a buggy. At a ranch house, you wait for others to arrive. Several men arrive with special explosives. You're given instructions how to use them. You are to mix some chemicals and then light a fuse.

Madame Peer goes over the map with you again. You realize that if you take a wrong turn you could explode the stuff under the town, instead of under the train tracks. You take careful note of that.

Soon you're crawling on hands and knees. You carry an oil lamp in one hand and explosives in a backpack.

Turn to page 88.

You reach the tracks so tired that you fall to the ground. You lie flat on your back, staring at the sun. You barely notice the sounds of an approaching train. You lift your head. The train not only slows down; it actually stops.

"There's the kid. I told you there was a kid over there." A heavy man in coveralls picks you up and carries you to the train. He hands you to a man he calls Charlie. Charlie places you on a bed in a passenger car.

"Where are you headed?" Charlie inquires.

"California," you whisper.

"We'll take care of that at the next station. Meanwhile, just relax. You might as well close your eyes. This is a long tunnel."

Once again you're in total blackout.

Turn to page 22.

With great effort you're soon back on the wagon. You hide among the boxes. The wagon pulls into a ranch and stops in a barn. You slip off and hide behind a pile of wood. After they unload the wagon and enter the house, you creep closer for a look inside. You eavesdrop on a conversation.

"Once we blow up those tunnels, no one will ever be able to leave. We'll be able to rule Heartland as our own little kingdom," a woman says.

"What about the army?"

"They can't get near unless they cross the granite divide. You can't get a horse across that," she replies.

You let it sink in and say to yourself, "If they blow up the tunnels, I'll never get to California—or home!" You crawl out from under the porch where you've been crouching. You run toward a saddled horse, trip, and grab a hanging rope. Too late you find out that the other end of the rope is attached to a dinner bell. A loud clang empties the house, just as you climb on the horse.

"Get that kid!" someone shouts.

A loud zipping noise sounds close by. You suddenly realize that they're shooting at you!

Turn to page 109.

At each junction, you stop to read the map and make sure you're going the right way. After a while you stop to rest. The tunnel is cool, and sounds travel great distances. In fact, you can faintly hear Madame Peer and Ruckman conversing at the tunnel entrance.

"How much longer?" he asks.

"About five minutes," she replies.

"How come you trust that kid?" Ruckman demands.

"Why not? What do we have to lose? The child's got no home, no parents, no one to come looking. . . . See what I mean? It's perfect. When the chemicals are mixed, pow! No tunnel. No time warp. No more interference. Just a floating bit of time and space in which we've got complete dominion and rule. . . ." She laughs in a hysterical kind of way.

"And no more kid," Ruckman adds.

"S'pose so. All that fuse business was nonsense. Once the two chemicals combine, it's all over."

Suddenly the tunnel is frightfully cold and creepy. A chill runs down your back. What are you going to do?

An idea begins to form in your mind.

Turn to page 99.

As you walk down the street, people run to hide behind closed doors. Women grab their children off the street. Grown men dive behind watering troughs. You turn a corner. An armed man faces you. A rifleman appears on a roof.

"That's far enough, Kid," he shouts. "You aren't going to the race today."

"Says who?" you bellow.

"Me and Mean Mountain Mike," he replies. "You're armed, and that means fair game."

"What? Oh, you mean this gun?" You reach for the gun to prove to them that it's not even loaded. A bullet just grazes your arm, and the gun drops to the ground.

"We've got you now, Kid," the roof man snarls. "Go on, Mike, finish the Kid off." The big man in the street, gun drawn, tramps closer.

"Look," you protest, "I'd rather not play this little game. Just let me go back to Chicago. I'm ready to go to Camp Winnachucka for the summer. I'll even put up with Cliffy McCracken," you ramble on, as the man continues to advance.

"This is all a dream, isn't it?" you continue. "Well, if it is a dream, I can do anything I want. Hey, Peewee," you shout at the approaching gunman. "You know any karate?" Fully convinced that this is just a nightmare you'll soon awaken from, you run for the big guy, leap in the air, and kick at whatever you can reach with your boots.

Turn to page 98.

Just as you crest the road, you see a mountain man trekking up the hill with his burro. You holler at him. It takes most of the afternoon for the two of you to carry the injured man up the canyon wall and into Heartland.

The doctor reports that the man will survive. He recognizes him as the owner of the Silver Dollar Hotel. The next day he is well enough to speak.

"Kid, you saved my life. How about becoming my partner in the hotel business? If it hadn't been for you, I'd have no use for the business at all. You take care of the bookwork; I'll handle the management. We'll split fifty-fifty. What do you say?" He sticks out a hand.

You feel very mature as you shake hands to ratify the deal.

"Out here," the doctor explains, "a man's only as good as his word. A handshake does it."

Later you walk over to the Silver Dollar. The owner introduces you to your hired help. After some instructions from an attorney, you sit down at a rolltop desk and examine the books. It feels good, like a shoe that fits well. You just know you are going to be in the hotel business for a long time.

THE END

You hang around for the picture, but it requires much effort to prevent the buffalo's wandering away. When you wanted it to get lost, it followed you. Now, when you want it to stick close by, it keeps getting lost.

Finally, Mrs. Edgars shows up with an old-fashioned box camera. She poses you with the little beast, and then she tosses a match in a pan of black powder. There's a flash. The picture is taken, but the buffalo stampedes away.

"Better not," Mrs. Edgars warns as you start to race after him. "One of the men will lasso him. Why don't you come down to the office and help put together tomorrow's edition?"

Several hours later the paper is done. The headline reads, "Buffalo Kid Booted Off Train."

"Buffalo Kid?" you retort.

"Why not? It does have a certain ring to it, don't you think?" Mrs. Edgars shows you how to bundle the papers. "Say, I like the way you help out. Would you like a job with the paper?"

"Only until I get enough money to go to California," you answer.

"That's fair."

Two months later Mrs. Edgars doesn't show up to work. A messenger boy from the hotel delivers a note instead: *I got a chance to work for the* St. Louis Dispatch. *Had to leave by stage immediately. It's all yours.*

The next day's edition reads, *The Buffalo Kid's Heartland Gazette.*

THE END

Two masked gunmen force a man in a dark business suit back on the train. "There's no stopping in Heartland this time, Judge. We don't need you here now."

A judge? Surely he'll know how to get you back on the train. You quickly design a plan of action. You climb a stack of barrels on the dock next to the train. You kick the top barrel with all your might. Two hundred and fifty pounds of dill pickles smash on the men below. You hope you missed the judge.

When the aftermath clears, the judge calls out, "Nice work! Let's go find the sheriff."

During lunch the judge tells you stories of his escapades in the Wild West. It sounds like something that happened long ago. He shows you his calendar—1885!

You laugh. "I know what this is. You've got one of those hidden cameras, right? Okay, where's the bald guy with the mike?"

The judge looks blank. "Have you got any relatives in these parts?" he finally asks.

You tell him about Chicago and trying to get to California.

"Well, if you've got folks in Chicago, I'll wire them. They can send you the money for a ticket."

"Yes, of course," you agree. Then you realize that if it really is 1885, your parents won't be alive.

Turn to page 138.

The Meat Menagerie is a steak house. You went to one once in Chicago. There are rough wooden tables and sawdust on the floor. There is no menu. But the waiter tells you about a moose steak dinner. You decide to try it.

The steak is delicious. The waiter brings your bill and you're astonished to read $1.00. "In Chicago I'd have to pay twenty dollars for a meal like that," you comment, reaching for your wallet.

You hand the man a dollar bill. He grabs your arm. "What's this? Confederate, or counterfeit?"

"It's real American money," you spout.

"It's real phony money, that's what. Look—it says 1981 on it. That's not even this century!"

You're getting concerned.

"We take only silver or gold," he concludes.

"Not traveler's checks?" you meekly suggest.

He yanks you by the collar. "Pay now, or else!"

Turn to page 118.

Everything is so confusing. You're in the wrong century, wanted for horse stealing, and have an opportunity to ride herd with real cowboys. *I wish I could talk to my dad,* you think.

Finally you blurt, "I'll go," to the man—who says he's called Wilson. "But I can't leave town a horse thief. The Lord won't give me any peace about that."

"So, you've got some religious upbringing," he says pleasantly. "That's just what this bunch needs. I got a Bible, but none of us can read too good."

"What about the horse-stealing charge?" you repeat.

"No problem. Just thump that gelding in the rear. It'll run right back to the livery. No way it will want to miss out on those oats."

"They won't arrest me?" you prod.

"Not if the horse makes it back. Besides, they won't follow you up here."

You ride into the trail camp behind Wilson. You're introduced around as the new wrangler. You discover that all a wrangler has to do is take care of the extra horses for the ten trail hands.

"How many horses are there?" you inquire.

"We've got 141 in the remuda now," Wilson explains. "We lost a couple swimming the North Platte."

"One hundred and forty-one horses!" You almost pass out.

Turn to page 140.

The next morning you buy a ticket to California. You board the train with a leather pouch full of gold coins to spare. "Won't the kids back home be surprised!" you say to yourself.

You bump into an old lady as you jostle down the aisle. Then, as you sit down, you're startled to notice the gold coins are no longer in your pocket. You dart to your feet.

"Hey, stop that lady!" you scream. "She's got my gold!"

Then everything goes black.

Turn to page 22.

Nothing happens. But someone thinks you're trying to kill the man. Arms grab to pull you off. You jerk away, and the force of the movement causes your clenched fists to jam even harder into the man's midsection. The man coughs, and a bone shoots out of his mouth. He gasps for air, but he is breathing.

After the danger passes, the grateful Mr. Way invites you to stay for a meal. As you eat, you tell him you're trying to get on the train.

"You just helped the right man," he says. "I happen to be general superintendent of the railroad."

After a delicious piece of berry pie, he takes you to the depot.

"Yessir," Mr. Way says as you watch the train roll in. "This is an exciting time to be alive. Just think, it won't be long till we have steam-driven buggies and automatic lights. Really, I see it coming. It's a good time to buy into a piece of the action. If I were you, I'd buy up some of that cheap land in California. But not around San Francisco—it's too expensive. Stay down in that little Spanish town called Los Angeles. Buy yourself a little farm. I guarantee it'll be worth something someday."

"If I don't make it back to the right century," you muse, "'I just might do that." As you settle back in the train car you daydream, "I wonder how much it would cost to buy all of Orange County?"

THE END

Just as you approach, Mean Mountain Mike lands a hard right hook to the shoulder of the mayor. He knocks the mayor out of the way of the oncoming stage. The lead horses, sensing danger, swerve at the last moment and avoid hitting Mean Mountain Mike. But you pass close enough for the girl to have an easy shot with the rope.

She catches the big man around the shoulders and arms and loops the other end of the rope around the brake handle of the stage. When the rope lets out all the way, it yanks Mean Mike to the ground and drags him along by the seat of his pants.

But the weight of the man forces the stage to slow down and stop. The whole town gathers around to congratulate you and the girl. The mayor finishes tying up the outlaw and several men carry him off to jail.

"How did you learn to drive a stage like that?" the mayor turns to you.

"It was nothing, sir," you reply with all truthfulness.

"Where's your family? I'd like to meet them," he continues. "Sissy and I owe you something."

Turn to page 105.

The heel of your boot connects full force with the man's chin. He sprawls out on his back. He's out cold and doesn't even wiggle.

"I've got this one." You look up to see the sheriff covering the man on the roof. "Now, go ahead and run your race."

Suddenly the streets fill with people. They almost carry you down to where a dozen riders wait by the corral. A man brings out a huge, well-groomed palomino horse for you.

"I knew you'd want Lightnin'," he says with a wink.

"Uh, sure," you reply, as you climb up on a fence post and mount the horse.

"And good luck on the suicide race," he adds.

"The what?" You hear a quiver in your voice.

Turn to page 104.

The old tunnel map shows a closed air vent that at one time opened a vertical shaft to bring fresh air down to the miners. You find the bottom of the shaft and ascend. It's a hard climb to where the shaft is closed. You attempt to remove rock to find your way out. Below, you hear shouts as Madame Peer and Ruckman inch their way into the tunnels after you.

"Ruckman! I'm stuck! Come help me!" you hear Madame Peer plead.

A thin beam of daylight breaks through the rocks above you. You scamper out of the mine onto the mountainside. You reach the entrance down the hill and see that both of them are still inside. The thought occurs to you that a well-timed toss of the explosives would blow up the mine entrance and lock Madame Peer and Ruckman inside.

Choices: **From the safety of a large boulder, you throw the glass jars of chemicals at the mine entrance (turn to page 103).**

You dump one jar in a sandpit and the other behind some old logs; then you walk back to town (turn to page 111).

A hot sun and tired body put you to sleep. When you awake, it's almost dark. You jump up to get down the mountain while you can see. You kick several boulders, which roll down the slope. As the noise diminishes, you hear a hissing sound, like a leaky bicycle tire.

"Snake!" you cry.

Too late. A hideous-looking diamondback clamps your flesh, and excruciating pain stabs your right leg. You kick and scream and fling the snake off into the canyon.

You desperately try to remember what to do. The sweat is pouring off you and the pain is unbearable. "Why didn't I pay more attention at the scout meeting!" you groan.

You try to walk, but you can't. Your head burns with fever. Nearby you hear a coyote howl as the night's first stars appear. "I've got to stay awake. I've got to make it," you tell yourself over and over. But the talking soon turns to mumbling. Then you hear nothing.

THE END

The cowboy shares his food and horse with you. As you travel along, he tells you about his life. It's kind of sad. No family, no real home, always on the move. He tries to make it sound exciting, but you're not so sure.

As you approach Stone Mountain Fort, a group of riders depart. The leader of the group, a man with a long, drooping mustache, beckons you and the cowboy to join them. You ride with this gang out of the mountains and down toward the tracks. A train is there. Looks like someone is carrying on some water.

You realize these men you're with intend to rob it. You feel very nervous about the whole thing.

Choices: You grab the cowboy's pistol and fire a warning shot (turn to page 102).
You wait, hoping to find a better opportunity to get away (turn to page 108).

The train crew hears your shot. The long train quickly moves again. By the time the outlaws reach the tracks, it's impossible for them to stop it. They all turn to you.

"So, you like to give warnings." The cowboy doesn't smile as kindly as he used to.

"I think it's time you did a little swinging," a man with a scar growls.

They toss a rope over a telegraph pole and fasten a hangman's noose. You try to explain. "You guys can't be serious. After all, I'm just a kid. Look, no one got hurt, right? You can't do this!" You're in tears as your voice rises.

They ignore you and place the noose over your neck.

"Wait, wait! I don't belong here. This is all a big mistake. I don't even know where I am!" you scream, almost incoherently.

"You won't be here long anyway," one of the men laughs, as he gives you a shove off your horse.

"Lord, help me," you pray.

Turn to page 106.

The explosion shatters the air. Rocks, tree branches, and dirt fly everywhere. You wait for the air to clear and your ears to stop ringing.

The mine entrance is buried in tons of rock. The earth beneath you vibrates violently. The explosion must have touched off an earthquake! You race for the prairie. The entire mountain feels as though it's collapsing.

You run for what seems to be miles and miles. A crowd of people from town have gathered to view the damage. You report the deaths of Madame Peer and Ruckman.

"Since you're her relative, that means you get all her businesses," the sheriff announces when you reach his office.

You start to protest, but the sheriff continues, "She owned the emporium and the general store. I suppose it's all yours, until we can find some other kin. But with the tunnel closed, it'll take months for new supplies. Guess you'll have to raise your prices right off."

You change your mind about informing him that you're not a relative. You'll wait and see first how you like being in business for yourself.

Worried customers line up right away. They pay big money for your merchandise. That night as you count your profits, a series of thoughts grips you. *I deserve this money. After all, I had to give up a lot to stay here. And who knows, maybe I am related to—*

Suddenly you hear a hideous, familiar laugh.

Turn to page 110.

Before the race, a Mr. Blackstrap instructs the riders. "I know some of you, like the Chicago Kid, know all about the race. But, for those who don't . . . you've got to ride across Lost Well Desert, over the granite mountain, swim the Big Rocky River (which is in flood stage this time of year); then it's down Dead Elk Canyon, back across the river, up the Indian Bow Trail, and into town. Remember, there are *no* other rules. Everything goes. I hope you all make it alive."

Before you can politely decline, a shot rings out. Someone slaps your horse, and you begin to fly through a rocky, cactus-strewn desert. You grab for the saddle horn and clutch the horse's mane instead. The horse seems to know the course. He dives off a cliff into some water. You close your eyes and hold your breath. The horse runs faster, as you hold on for dear life.

When you're brave enough to open your eyes, you see you're approaching the town. You yell for someone to stop your horse, but no one hears. The crowd goes wild as the palamino crosses the finish line. He comes to an abrupt halt, and you sail over his head, turn a summersault in midair, and miraculously land on your feet. The audience loves it. All you know is that your white-knuckled hands still grasp two handfuls of horsehair.

"You were terrific, Kid," someone cheers from the mob.

"Shucks, it was nothin', ma'am," you reply.

Turn to page 112.

You remember your need to get to California.
You ask the mayor for help in returning to the
train.

"No problem," he says.

Sissy looks disappointed. "I thought we might
take on some other adventures," she says. "We
made such a good team."

"Like what did you have in mind?" you ask.

"Going out to the Lucky J Mine. I'd like to nose
around to discover why they keep hiring more
men when they claim they've found no gold. I
suspect something."

"And you think I could help you find out?"

"Sure," she laughs. "Kids can get away with a
lot. I ought to know."

Choices: You turn down her offer, and investigate the next available train (turn to
page 120).

You can always go to California later.
You go with Sissy to the Lucky J Mine
(turn to page 144).

A thunderous discharge rips the still air. The rope is shattered, and you hit the ground. The outlaws begin shooting. But when they see approaching horses, they head for the hills.

Two riders dismount. One is an Indian who carries a rifle and wears buckskin. The other is a tall man with a white horse and a white hat. He wears a black mask over his eyes. You don't care whether he's an outlaw or not, he just saved you from hanging.

"Tonto," the tall man says, "You take the youngster to the next train stop. I'll track the renegades to make sure they don't double back."

Suddenly the man is gone.

"Who was that masked man?" you ask the Indian.

Turn to page 124.

The outlaws surround the train. You notice one of them pulling dynamite out of a saddlebag.

Whoever is in the baggage car refuses to open the door, so the outlaws tie a dozen sticks of dynamite to it and light the fuse. You hear a man shouting from inside the car. He has no idea what's about to happen.

You run up close to him and yell, "Get away! They're blowing up the door!"

As you turn to flee, a roar blasts you into space.

Turn to page 121.

You head for a steep ridge of mountains to the north. You look back to see puffs of dust. They're following you. As you climb the granite hills, you have to abandon your horse and continue by foot. The four men trailing behind do the same. Should you just hide? Keep climbing? You decide to continue on.

You keep an eye on the men. They have their guns drawn. You crest the mountain ridge and race downhill as fast as you can. Soon you're out of control. You couldn't stop if you wanted to.

Bullets whiz behind you. You smack right into a tree. "Lord, deliver me from the hands of my enemy," you pray, remembering a verse from Sunday school.

In the distance, you hear a strange noise. You stretch your bruised body to listen. It sounds like a horn . . . like a bugle! You hear the hoofbeats of many riders and a few moments look up to see . . .

"The cavalry! It's the cavalry!" you shout at the top of your lungs. "Never mind, Lord," you add. "The cavalry's here!"

Turn to page 126.

The laugh is terrifying because it is your own.

THE END

When you get to town, you tell the sheriff about the plan to blow up the tunnel. He takes a posse and rides out to the mountain. Before nightfall Madame Peer and her henchmen are all behind bars. The town is in a joyous mood.

As a reward for the arrest of Madame Peer, the sheriff offers you ownership of her stores. "They're all yours," he explains. "Do with them whatever you want."

"I just want a ticket to California," you plead.

"You've got it," he replies, "But what about these stores?"

"Give them . . . give them to . . ." you look around at the crowd and pause. Then you point to a Chinese family in an old wagon. "Give them to that family."

"What? Er . . . okay. So be it," the sheriff answers. The people all cheer.

The first thing next morning you board the train for California, and it seems like half the town sees you off. The Chinese family gratefully bow and exclaim excitedly. Unfortunately, you do not understand a word they say.

The train travels a distance out of town, and you begin to relax. You relive your unbelievable experiences and sigh to yourself, *And to think, it all started when we entered a tunnel.*

Then everything goes black.

Turn to page 22.

"Come on, Kid, it's time for the wild bull riding," a man with a blue-checkered shirt urges.

"You *are* going to ride Old Thunder, ain't you?" another encourages. They both wait for an answer.

They don't get one. You're flat on your back in a dead faint.

THE END

"Actually, these aren't my clothes; see, I was just heading to a Sunday school meeting, and . . ." You try to talk your way out of it.

"A Sunday school meeting? Are you loco?" he shouts.

"No, really . . . It's a very good thing to attend, . . . You know we all need to learn as much about God as we can. Wouldn't you say so? Perhaps you'd like to join me." You try to sound confident, but you aren't sure that the diversion will calm the gunman. "I have no intention of racing on this day, or any day," you assert.

"The Chicago Kid's got religion!" the man on the roof shouts down to a huge man walking up the street. Both of them double up with laughter, and you hurry back to try to find the Sunday school teacher.

You put on your own clothes at the depot storeroom and ask around for the teacher. She looks happy that you found her.

Turn to page 129.

Your bullet misses the man badly, but it hits a cast-iron weather vane atop the building. The shot then bounces off and strikes the man in the arm—causing him to drop his rifle. A huge man is angrily running toward you all this time, but the rifle discharges when it hits the ground. The bullet strikes the man in the leg. Both wounded men cry out in pain and beg you not to shoot them again.

"The Chicago Kid got them both with one bullet!" a little girl yells as people start to flood back into the street. Soon you are riding a beautiful big palamino through happy crowds of people.

"I'm counting on you winning the race!" a man shouts at you.

"What race?" you ask.

"Why, the suicide race, of course," he says with a grin.

Turn to page 104.

It takes awhile, but you find both shoes; then you climb to the top of the canyon and the roadway. You notice that the man under the wagon hasn't moved. "I just know he's dead," you say to yourself.

But you aren't convinced.

As you hike up a hill, you notice that the gold coins are very heavy. Every time you think of them, you envision the injured man on the side of the canyon. Finally the weight of the coins, combined with the weight of your guilt, becomes unbearable. You sling the coins down and run to the top of the hill, and are surprised at what you see.

Turn to page 90.

"There's been a terrible mistake," you tell the ticket agent. "I was put off the train in the wrong place; I need to get to California."

You give the agent your name, and he checks his records. "You're right," he says, "your name isn't on the list of those who are to get off in Heartland. In fact, your name isn't on the list of paying passengers. You must be a stowaway, and you sure aren't getting back on this train."

Not knowing what to do, you start walking down the tracks toward the west. It is almost dark when you get to a tunnel entrance in a sheer rock cliff. There is no way you can climb over it or go around it. You decide to take your chances and walk through the tunnel. About halfway through, you lose your balance and start to fall. Instead of hitting the tracks, you start spinning around and around. You are brought back to earth with a thud as you hit the ground outside the tunnel. While you lie there

trying to figure out what's happening, you see lights in the distance, and then . . .

"HEADLIGHTS!" you shout. "It's a real car!"

A man and a woman get out of a late-model pickup and come to your assistance. "Child, are you hurt?"

"You've got a pickup . . . and flashlights . . . and you're wearing tennis shoes, and . . . and . . . is this the 1980s?" you stammer.

"Must be some head injuries, Aaron," the lady says softly.

"Fell out of the train, I suppose," the man replies. "Well, let's not just stand here. We've got to get the kid to a hospital emergency room and call the parents. How's that sound to you, kid?"

"Nothing ever sounded better," you sigh. "Nothing ever sounded better."

THE END

"But it's all the money I have. . . ." You frantically search your mind for a solution.

"Give me the funny watch you have strapped to your arm," he suggests.

"Well, actually it's a caculator watch and was a present." Once again you are interrupted.

"What kind of watch?" he asks, puzzled.

"Calculator. It adds, subtracts, multiplies, divides, and does elementary calculus in addition to . . ."

"No kidding? Show me how it works." The man looks more curious than angry now.

"Well," you continue, "suppose I wanted to find out what fifteen times fifteen is."

"Two twenty-five," he inserts.

"I mean, suppose I didn't know that. I would just punch in fifteen times fifteen and hit the equal button. There—225."

He looks amazed. "And it divides, too?"

"Sure," you confidently reply.

"I could use one of those. Say, kid, tell you what I'll do. I'll give you the meal, plus, er . . . let's say . . . that pinto Spanish pony out front for that fancy watch of yours."

At first you are tempted. It's not every day you can trade a watch for a horse. But then you realize that you couldn't take a pony on the train.

"I don't reckon you have much of a choice, kid. I want my pay." He reaches for your watch.

Then you remember your grandpa's present. "Wait!" you yell.

Turn to page 139.

Your time as a deputy passes quickly, and soon you have the routine down smoothly. Heartland is quiet most of the time, so you have time to learn how to ride, rope, and shoot the six-gun that you carry at your hip.

Then one night it happens.

A tough cowboy named Lance refuses to let you check his gun. He forces you out to the street, and others dive for cover. There's no way out but to disarm him.

"Lance, for the last time—give me that gun," you bravely say.

"Never, Kid. You'll have to fight me for it," he growls.

He goes for his gun at the same time you reach for yours. But a terrifying shot rings out before you even clear the leather.

Turn to page 141.

As you head out of town on the train the next morning you keep thinking about all your adventures.

"Life is going to seem pretty dull from now on," you say with a sigh.

THE END

You come to in the passenger car of a moving train. The conductor is standing near you.

"You saved my life, kid. If you wouldn't have warned me I could have been blown up. I can't thank you enough. Sure we lost some money, but we didn't have much. Listen, where do you want to go? I'll give you a free ride anywhere."

"Just get me to California," you reply weakly.

"You got it, kid. Now just relax, we're about to enter a long, cool tunnel," he assures.

Once again the lights go out.

This time there is no explosion.

Turn to page 22.

You run from the wagon and through the hills. From the trail of dust, you realize the driver hasn't even noticed that you are gone. Not knowing where to head, you aim for some tall trees in the distance. You suppose they are near a river.

You're right about the water. But the trees also hold a family of Indians. As you approach with caution, you notice a great wailing and commotion by the riverbank. When you get close enough to see, you notice that a little Indian girl must have drowned. Her parents are panicked, trying to revive the limp little body.

You rush right by several Indian children and immediately begin to apply artificial respiration just as you saw them do on an educational TV show.

The girl's father starts to grab you, but the mother says something you don't understand, and they leave you alone. You pray as you try to

get the girl's lungs working on their own. Suddenly she coughs out a lungful of brackish water and gasps for breath. Then she starts crying. The Indians rejoice, grabbing their daughter and dancing around you.

"Little one has big medicine!" the father replies. "You have family?"

"Yeah, er . . . no. Not here . . ." You don't know how to explain.

"Now you part of my family. I'll call you Little Healer. From now on you live with Indians, travel with Indians, become one with Indians." He doesn't wait for a reply.

Somehow, it all makes sense to you. Like this was where you had been headed all along. *Well,* you think to yourself, *it won't be a dull life.*

THE END

"If I told you, you wouldn't believe it," the Indian says with a smile.

You ride behind him all the way into town. He takes you to the train depot but you find out you will have to wait until the next day for another train. Before he leaves you, he gives you several bullets and says you can use them for money.

You stand at the depot platform, staring at the bullets. You aren't sure how they could be worth anything, so you go up to the man at the counter. He's talking to a lady with some children. When he finishes, you ask, "Mister, are these bullets worth anything?"

He pulls out his knife and scratches one of them. "Son, where did you get these? They're solid silver!"

One of the children hears the conversation and comes over to you with wonder in his eyes. "There's only one man in the West that uses silver bullets. Do you know the Lone Rang—"

"Do I know him?" you interrupt. "Let me tell you how he saved my life."

All of a sudden you notice that everyone in the depot has stopped talking and is straining to hear what you are about to say. You like being the center of attention, so you stretch the story out to make it last. By the time you get to the part where the noose explodes and the masked rider appears, the whole crowd breaks into wild applause.

The ticket agent slaps you on the back and invites you to go home with him for dinner. You accept the invitation.

"Maybe you'd like to stay in Heartland. At least until he brings in those would-be train robbers," the agent says. "Then you could talk with him some more."

"I think I'll do that," you say. "I think I'll just do that."

THE END

Soon your attackers are rounded up. A lieutenant lets you ride behind him as you grimace from your wounds. "Sorry, kid, we can't take you into town. We have to get right back to the fort. But I will leave you at Meadow Creek Junction. You should be able to hitch a ride into town from there."

You wash up in the cool clear water of Meadow Creek and wait for a ride towards town. Soon a bright red painted wagon comes up the road, heading toward the prairie. Two men are driving, and on the side, in slightly peeling paint, are the words "RAINMAKER—Reasonable Rates." They stop the wagon and you run over to talk to them about a ride. You tell them your whole story.

"You say the cavalry saved you?" the short one asks.

"Yes, I was just getting ready to pray and then the cavalry came and I—"

"Well, kid, I'd say your prayers were an-

swered. There ain't no cavalry within 1200 miles of here." He laughs as he finishes.

"No, really," you insist. "The cavalry came and the lieutenant brought me here."

"They rode by here, eh?" he asks.

"Yeah, all one hundred of them. Right over by that cottonwood tree." You point.

The three of you walk over to the trees. The ground around it is smooth and soft, but there isn't one single horse track!

"Well, kid, I don't read much sign," the short man continues, "but there hasn't been a horse around here since the last rain." He turned to the taller man. "Ain't kids something? Making up stories about the cavalry. Almost had me believing him!"

You climb into the wagon and ride between the men. *No cavalry? Then who saved me?* you ponder as you ride.

Turn to page 145.

The cloth keeps you from getting cut, and you run back toward the train depot. Not knowing whether or not anyone is chasing you, you dart through the depot's storeroom door that you had so recently bypassed.

It takes a moment for your eyes to get accustomed to the light.

Turn to page 24.

"I'm happy to have you help me," she says matter-of-factly.

You didn't know you had volunteered.

"We'll have a week of meetings here and then go to California. Missionaries go for free on the trains, you know," she says.

You suddenly realize that this is your way out of this crazy town, so you agree to stay and help.

She puts you in charge of the littlest children. You enjoy the time since they have never heard any Bible stories at all. You actually hate to see the week come to an end. On Friday evening there is a big program, and many of the parents come to hear the teacher. They commit themselves to building a permanent Sunday school and church in Heartland. It's exciting to think that you had a vital part in bringing the good news about Jesus to this town.

Saturday morning, as you two board the train, a committee of townspeople shows up and asks if you won't stay through the summer and teach their families all about the Bible.

The Sunday school teacher wants to stay, but you tell her you have to get to your aunt's house. She says, "You know we all have some unique service to complete for the Lord, and it doesn't always come about in the way we expect. Don't spend the rest of your life being sorry you failed to hear his call."

In a strange way, what she says makes sense to you. You agree to stay.

THE END

You made a slight miscalulation. They are not firecrackers, but rockets! When they blow, they shoot off in your direction. Six big rockets shooting gold sparks and flames head right towards you. In panic you take a couple steps and then dive into a horse watering trough for safety. When you come out of the water you hear the boys laughing at you.

But only for a moment.

The rockets bounced off the water tower and crashed right through the roof of the little fireworks shed out back. It is the most beautiful blast in the world. Brilliant greens, blues, golds, reds, and silvers flash in every direction. It is like a ballet of the sun for your personal viewing pleasure.

The whole town gathers around the little building to watch. When the last spray finally goes out, and there is nothing left but a smoldering building, everyone becomes very quiet.

"Who set those off?" someone shouts.

You try to hide in the crowd, but the two boys point you out.

"The wet kid with the funny shoes," they reveal.

Then suddenly there is a loud round of cheers and applause. "It was the greatest show ever!" "Nice job, kid!"

"Haven't had this much fun in years!"

"Let's appoint the kid to set them off every year!"

You tell them you have to get to California, and they walk with you to the train. You walk triumphantly past the two boys. Even the conductor tips his hat to you. You relax as the train pulls away. That's when you notice two things.

First, your clothes are almost dry now.

Second . . . somebody turned out the lights!

Turn to page 22.

You walk slowly up a hill in the direction, you hope, of town. Your feet hurt, and you stop at the crest of a hill to rest. That's when you notice an old mountain man with his mules, next to a log cabin in the woods. The man spots you.

"You lost, kid?" he questions.

"I sure am. Really lost. I'm suppose to be in California," you reply.

"You headed for Californy? Think you'll need some shoes." He laughs and pulls a beautiful pair of beaded moccasins out of his pack. "Come on along and help me bring down a few head of buffalo, and I'll see that you get on a train to Californy. And just for good measure, you can have them pair of moccasins."

Since you don't have any good alternatives, you decide to go with the mountain man for a while. As he makes camp that night, you listen to many exciting stories about the man's life and travels. As you're drifting off to sleep you ask, "How long will it take to get the buffalo?" You're hoping it won't be more than a day or two.

"Oh, we'll be finished by Christmas," he states without hesitation.

"Christmas! I'll be out here 'till Christmas?" you croak.

"Provided we don't get snowed in, or captured by Indians . . . but that's what makes life exciting," he says with a grin.

There doesn't seem to be much chance of your life getting dull for some time.

THE END

Two of the outlaws charge toward you. You're still flat on your back, trying to catch your breath. "What happened to you, kid?" they demand.

You think fast. "I've been staying with a Chinese family, and, well, do you happen to know the symptoms for bubonic plague? I don't feel so good."

"Plague?"

"Yeah, the bubonic plague."

"The kid does look sick," says one.

"Yeah, about to die," adds the other. They back off. You hear them run for their horses, mount, and leave. You whoop with delight just as the Chinese girl climbs down the hill. She grabs you and hugs you and chatters away.

The two of you hike back to her family. By dark you reach Heartland and find the doctor to look at the father's wounds. The next morning you have no problem getting a ticket at the depot, as the railroad company is delighted with the help they received the day before.

You wave to your new friends as the train pulls out. You sit back and doze awhile. When you awake, everything is inky dark.

Turn to page 22.

When you come to, the train is out of sight and the Chinese girl is struggling to get her hands free. Soon she has you both untied.

"How did that happen?" you ask. She doesn't respond. You grab her arm and try to get her to understand. "Train . . . zoom! . . . us . . . necks? . . . no crunchee? What happened?"

"Oh," she says with a nod, "Jesus saves!"

You shake your head in frustration, and she takes you by the hand and leads you up the hill about twenty feet. There she points to a parallel train track that was hidden from sight by brush and weeds. She walks you back down the hill and shows you a train switch. You had been tied to a siding and neither you or the train robbers knew it. Only trains stopping for more water use the siding.

"Jesus saves!" the young girl exclaims again.

"Whew!" you sigh. "He sure does . . . he sure does!"

You decide the train ride can wait. The last thing you want to see is another train. You go back with the girl to locate her father, and to learn from her more about trusting the Lord. You figure it will be worth your time.

THE END

After a long afternoon of play practice, you try on the costume. It fits fine. By curtain time you're actually looking forward to the performance.

You blow a few lines, but the actor covers for you. The townspeople love it. Even the second-rate acting entertains them. They rise to their feet for thunderous ovations.

After the last scene of the day, you and the actor order the largest steak in the hotel dining room. "You know," the man tells you, "I like the way you act. How about finishing this tour with me?"

You perk up. "Where are we going?"

"All the big towns," he beams. "Virginia City, Silver City, Tombstone, even California."

"California," you almost shout. "Whereabouts?"

"San Bernardino," he replies.

"That's close enough," you say with enthusiasm. "And now, I'd like a piece of berry pie. How about you, partner?"

THE END

"I'm going to wait for Mr. Russell and the rodeo," you explain to Mrs. Edgars. She marches off to the bank.

Mr. Russell brings another man to tell you what to do. They dress you in leather and moccasins and show you how to do an Indian dance.

It's more like a Wild West show than a rodeo. There's trick shooting and roping, followed by a melodrama, some bronc riding, and a man who rides a humpbacked bull. Then you and the baby buffalo dance around. Everyone cheers.

At the end of the show, Mr. Russell tosses you a silver dollar and asks if you'd like to go on tour with them. You not only decline, but you give him the buffalo. As you walk back through the town flipping your silver dollar, you notice a cafe called the Hong Kong Noodle Company.

You walk inside. It's like walking into another world.

Turn to page 72.

Sudddenly you remember a name from stories your grandmother used to tell about *her* grandfather. *Thank you, Lord,* you rejoice.

"Listen, Judge, my grandfather is Zebulon P. Courtland of Franklin Grove, Illinois. If you'd wire him, maybe he'd send me some train fare. Tell him I'm going to be . . . I mean, I'm a grandson on Eleta's side of the family."

It takes three days to hear back from Illinois. The telegram reads, "Dear Judge, I'm sending the money. I'm crazy to do it, but somehow the Lord keeps telling me I should. Tell the youngster to fabricate a better story next time. Eleta's only three years old. Signed, Zeb Courtland."

By the time you board the train to California, a whole week has zoomed by. You're dizzy thinking about it. An ancient town from out of the past, and a kind man who sent money to someone who claimed to be a future relative.

A businessman stares down at your shoes. "Hey, here's another pair of those funny shoes," he roars. "Saw a kid on the train last week wearing the same thing."

You smile sweetly and say, "They're the latest thing."

THE END

You reach behind some pictures and next to your library card in your wallet. You've had the genuine silver dollar so long you'd forgotten it was real money. Grandpa said when he'd given it to you, "Hang on to it. It'll be worth something someday." You glance at the date: 1883.

"Wow, I just made it," you say under your breath. You hand the coin to the man and tell him you know it's worth over $25, because it's so old.

"It's only two years old, and it's worth a dollar like the rest," he says indignantly.

You walk to the station and show the agent your computer watch. Once he sees how it'll help him with his work, he's anxious to trade a ticket to California for it. In fact, he personally escorts you to your seat and shows everyone on the train the new watch. He gets off and waves good-bye to you; then he shouts as the train pulls out, "Hey, kid, how do I wind this thing?"

"Ohhh," you groan, "you need a battery."

"Battery? What's a battery?" he shouts as the train speeds away.

THE END

"Don't worry," Wilson assures you, "Cookie, here, will train you."

And he does. Over the next several weeks you're amazed at how much horsemanship you learn. But the best times are evenings around the fire. The whole camp listens as you read from the Bible.

"We've been gone from south Texas since late March. Most times here on the prairie we've got nothing to do but think and ride. Some new ideas will do us good," Wilson explains.

A few of the men sleep through the readings, but the others insist you continue. Once, while you camp by a tiny northern Montana town, four of the crew approach you. "Hey, kid, Wilson says we can go into town this morning. We wondered if you'd go with us. We want to go to church."

As you sit in the tiny log church and listen to a "fire and brimstone" sermon, the thought dawns on you, *Maybe this is why the Lord plopped me down in another century. Just to help these men understand him better.*

During the prayer time you release your worries on the Lord. "Father, it seems I should be back in the twentieth century with my family. But if you want me here, I'm glad to have you work through me."

THE END

You don't feel anything. "He missed!" you think. Then, you realize that Lance is the one who fell. "But I didn't . . ."

You turn to see the sheriff standing with a gun still smoking. "I did," he says. "I knew you weren't fast enough. Maybe you're right. Maybe you should ride on out to California."

You insist that he keep you on as deputy. But the sheriff won't hear it. The next morning he pays you your back wages in gold coins. "You tried really hard, but the job just doesn't fit you."

You eye the coins. "Well, at least I'll have a tangible memory of all this," you tell yourself.

Turn to page 95.

142

"Doc Haney! Doc Haney!" you call out wildly.

An elderly man with a walking stick yells back, "Doc rode out of town about half an hour ago."

You rush back to the hotel. A circle of people crowd around the nearly dead man who can barely breathe. "Let me through, let me through," you shout. "I know what to do . . ."

Some big hands grab you and hold you back. "Keep that kid back," someone snaps. You manage to free yourself and stumble headfirst onto the gasping Mr. Way. Your head strikes him a bit below the rib cage. The man coughs hard and breathes air. The force of your blow dislodges a bone from his throat.

"Are you a lucky man, Mr. Way," says one of the waitresses. "That child fell on you . . ."

"I don't believe in luck, ma'am," Mr. Way inserts. "Must have been the good Lord's design. I've been putting off retirement for years. I keep saying, 'Lord, if you want me to move to Idaho and be a missionary to the Indians, you'll have to give me a sign.' This must be it." He turns to you. "Thanks for saving my life."

Missionary? Your being here may start a missionary movement?

The grateful Mr. Way accompanies you to the train and waves as you leave Heartland. You remember a book in the church library back home about missionaries in the west. You can hardly wait to find out if there's one named Way. But, first, into the tunnel . . .

Turn to page 22.

As the two of you ride out of town toward the Lucky J, you discuss what to call your team.

"How about Sissy and The Kid," she suggests.

"Sure," you laugh. "It won't make any difference. No one will remember us anyway."

You are wrong.

From 1885 until 1903, there are no better range detectives than Sissy and The Kid.

THE END

Now it's the big man's turn to talk. "Kid, we're not headed to town. At least, not for a while. There are a few farmers out west of here we need to see. We'd be happy if you'd join us. After all, we could use someone with an imagination like yours."

"But I don't know anything about rainmaking!" you protest.

"You got the best part of it down already," the little man says with a smile. "Now all you have to do is learn to beat the drum. I suppose you'll learn that in time."

THE END

"Well," the mayor says, putting his arm around you. "Now that you've handled Mike, you shouldn't have any problems with Little Antelope."

"Who?"

"You know, Little Antelope, Chief of the Wasatch Indians. He and several braves came riding into town all decked out in war paint, shouting about how we broke the treaty."

Half dragging you down the street, the mayor pushes you into a large barn. "I'm sure you'll have just the right words to say. Don't worry, Governor," he continues as he shuts the door behind you. "We'll all be right out here behind you."

As your eyes become accustomed to the dark barn you see a dozen large Indians with knives drawn, standing around you. You manage a weak smile and finally lift your hand and say, "How. Me friend."

"That, trembling Governor," the one with the blue feather in his hat says, "remains to be seen."

You figure you're in for a long, hard day. You're right.

THE END

❧ PARENTS ❧

Are you looking for fun ways to bring the Bible to life in the lives of your children?

Chariot Family Publishing has hundreds of books, toys, games, and videos that help teach your children the Bible and apply it to their everyday lives.

Look for these educational, inspirational, and fun products at your local Christian bookstore.

A Making Choice Book

THE ISLAND MANSION MYSTERIES
by Janet Bly

Get ready for the adventure of a lifetime!

You're off to Hawaii to present your prize-winning computer game to an international corporation. You'll have three days of hot sun and pounding surf, and maybe a big contract. Unless, that is, your visit is disrupted by . . .

- ✓ a kidnapper in a helicopter,
- ✓ a volcano that's ready to blow, or
- ✓ a madman's threat to the peace of the islands.

Making Choices Books let you create your own stories with the choices you make page by page. If you don't like the way things are turning out in your story, you can go back and start over. There are more than thirty possible endings!

Best of all, you'll find out how the choices you make can affect the rest of your life . . . and that God really cares about the choices you make.

You'll find this and other **Making Choices Books** at your local Christian bookstore.

Time Warp Tunnel .ISBN 0-7814-0187-9

The Island Mansions Mysteries . . . . . .ISBN 0-7814-0191-7

Chariot Books™
A Division of Cook Communications

The Pet That Never Was

"What are you bringing to show and tell, T.J.?"

His mom is coming up the stairs, his best friend, Zack, is stuck in a tree just outside the window of his third-story bedroom, and the rest of the guys are waiting at the front door to see an eight-foot pet boa constrictor that T.J. doesn't have and never did.

How could one innocent question land T.J. in so much trouble?

Timothy John Fairbanks, Jr., is your typical kid next door. Through the adventures in which he continually finds himself, T.J. learns what it means to rely on God. With the help of his parents, he discovers how God can help him deal with even the worst of problems.

You can read all about **T.J.**, by Nancy Simpson Levene, in:

Look for T.J. at your local Christian bookstore.

Chariot Books™
A Division of Cook Communications

Just give me another chance.

That's all Everett wanted—another chance to be Chuck's friend. To prove he wasn't the yellow belly coward Chuck said he was. But Chuck wasn't about to give Everett a chance to prove anything.

His mom said pray. The Lord would work it out. Well, he didn't see the Lord doing much of anything. Did He even care about Everett?

But one day at the abandoned house across Rocky Creek, Everett would get his second chance, and a chance to know God did care about him. Would he be able to prove to his friends and himself he wasn't a coward? Or would he blow it again?

You'll want to read all the **Rocky Creek Adventure** books by Mark Littleton, available at your local Christian bookstore:

Chariot Books™
A Division of Cook Communications